He was tempted. So tempted.

How many times over the years had his thoughts strayed to Bree and where she was and what she was doing? And then to have her practically dropped into his lap by a weird twist of fate and weather...

She looked almost exactly the way she had when she was his. It was hard for his brain and his body to recognize that was no longer the case. When his fingertips brushed across her pink mouth, her lips had parted seductively, nearly begging him to kiss her. And he'd wanted to. Man, he'd wanted to.

Which was why he walked away. Why he had to stay away from Bree Harper.

* * *

Snowed In with Her Ex
is part of the Brides and Belles series—
Wedding planning is their business...and their pleasure.

* * *

If you're on Twitter,
tell us what you think of Harlequin Desire!
#harlequindesire

Dear Reader,

I love weddings. I do. Give me a marathon of *Say Yes to the Dress* or *Platinum Weddings* and I can waste a whole day. There's just something about the moment—bringing together all the important people in your life to celebrate love. I enjoy every detail, from choosing table linens and cake flavors to offering guests signature cocktails and a fun after-party where they can dance and enjoy themselves. Sometimes I think if I wasn't in the romance-writing business, I'd get into the wedding-planning business.

The beauty of being a writer is that I can experience other careers through my characters. With this new Brides and Belles miniseries, I'll finally get to fill my need for wedding fabulousness. All that time watching David Tutera will finally pay off—it's research!

At From This Moment, the wedding company featured in the book, the four women who started the company each have their specialties. Bree is the photographer, the artist and the shunner of technology. She's passionate about her art and following her dream, so of course I bring back the man from her past who walked away from his own dreams and trap them in a cabin during a blizzard. It doesn't take long for the heat these two put off to melt the ice.

If you enjoy Ian and Bree's story, tell me by visiting my website at www.andrealaurence.com, like my fan page on Facebook or follow me on Twitter. I'd love to hear from you!

Enjoy,

Andrea

SNOWED IN
WITH HER EX

—

ANDREA LAURENCE

To Perrin —
Thanks for being
awesome!

Andrea
Laurence

H HARLEQUIN® DESIRE

Recycling programs
for this product may
not exist in your area.

ISBN-13: 978-0-373-73362-0

Snowed In with Her Ex

Printed in U.S.A.

www.Harlequin.com

Andrea Laurence is an award-winning contemporary romance author who has loved books and has been writing stories since she learned to read and write. She always dreamed of seeing her work in print and is thrilled to be able to share her books with the world. A dedicated West Coast girl transplanted into the Deep South, she's working on her own happily-ever-after with her boyfriend and five fur-babies. You can contact Andrea at her website, www.andrealaurence.com.

Books by Andrea Laurence

Harlequin Desire

Brides and Belles series

Snowed In with Her Ex

Millionaires of Manhattan series

What Lies Beneath
More Than He Expected
His Lover's Little Secret

Secrets of Eden series

Undeniable Demands
A Beauty Uncovered
Heir to Scandal
Her Secret Husband

Visit Andrea Laurence's profile at Harlequin.com for more titles.

Prologue

"I'm sorry." Briana Harper interrupted her business partner in the middle of their weekly meeting. "Did you just say we've booked the Missy Kline and Ian Lawson wedding? *The* Missy Kline and Ian Lawson?"

Natalie, the wedding planner and office manager, looked up from her tablet, her brow furrowing in mild irritation at Bree breaking her flow. "Yes," she said with a heavy sigh. "What's the big deal with that? We have plenty of celebrity weddings."

Bree shook her head and returned to tapping absently at her own tablet. "I'm just surprised, that's all." That wasn't all, but she wasn't going to tell her best friends and business partners that. One of the most important rules at From This Moment was to remain professional at all times. It didn't matter if the ring bearer knocked over the wedding cake, a guest spoke up during the dreaded "if anyone has any reason why these two should not be wed" moment or the groom was your ex-boyfriend. So Bree kept her mouth shut.

"They're all over the magazine covers at the grocery store checkout lines," Gretchen added. "I don't know how you could've missed it. Apparently she's pregnant, too."

"I guess I've been eating too much takeout," Bree muttered. Pregnant. The bare-midriff pop queen was going to have Ian's baby. For some reason that bothered her. A lot. How could she have missed this news?

Natalie flung her dark brown hair over her shoulder and continued on with her Monday morning briefing. When Natalie was focused on the job, there was no room for joking around or unnecessary drama.

Each Monday, the four owners of From This Moment met to discuss new clients, business issues and the previous weekend's wedding.

From This Moment was a one-stop wedding venue that catered to the discriminating Nashville bride. Anybody who was anybody got married at their facility. In just six short years, college friends Natalie, Amelia, Gretchen and Bree had gone from being nobodies with a dream to members of the Nashville business elite.

Together, they were a powerhouse of wedding perfection. If they couldn't do it, they knew someone who could. Anything the bridal couple wanted, they made it happen. No request was too complex, and they built a reputation on that. That, and a policy of strict confidentiality.

Natalie was right; they did have their fair share of celebrities marry here. Missy Kline was just one more star they could add to their roster of famous clients, but Bree couldn't care less about her. She was far more interested in Missy's groom—Nashville music producer and owner of SpinTrax Records, Ian Lawson.

Once upon a time, Ian had been the center of Bree's universe. They had met as freshmen at Belmont University in Nashville and for more than a year, they had been inseparable. He had been the sexy coffee shop musician with the long hair in his sleepy eyes and the smile that could charm her panties off. When he'd played his guitar and sang to her, all was right in the world. And then he had stopped playing and everything went wrong.

"Bree?"

Bree's head snapped up. The other three ladies were looking at her. She'd obviously missed something. "Yes?"

"I said," Natalie repeated, "will you be able to do the engagement portraits this Thursday and still be back in time to cover the rehearsal dinner for the Conner wedding on Friday?"

Now it was Bree's turn to frown. "Why wouldn't I be back in time? It only takes a couple hours for an engagement shoot."

"The bride wants to do the photo shoot at the groom's cabin in Gatlinburg." Amelia repeated the detail Bree had missed.

"That should be fine."

"Okay, good." Natalie made a note. "I'll get you the address of the cabin. Plan to arrive around noon."

That was that. Once Natalie noted something in her tablet, it was virtually signed in blood. There was no getting out of it now. Bree would finally come face-to-face with the man who had haunted her thoughts and dreams for the past nine years.

And his new bride.

One

"This is not good."

As though the universe had heard Ian's words, the tires on his Cadillac Escalade skidded on a patch of ice. He corrected the truck's erratic movement and steered it back into the lane and away from the deep ditch on the side of the road. Gripping the leather steering wheel with white-knuckled tension, he cursed and silently thanked his assistant for making sure he left first thing this morning. Any later and he might not have made it.

The snowflakes were growing increasingly difficult to see through and were collecting along the side of the road. On the freeway from Nashville toward Gatlinburg, the weather had changed from rain to sleet to an icy slush. Now, in the heart of the Smoky Mountains, it was one hundred percent snow.

And a lot of it.

At the bottom of the hill that led to his mountainside

community, he backed up slightly, put his SUV into a lower gear and started accelerating up the incline. Slow and steady, he made it up and around the long, winding curve to his driveway at the very top, then pulled into the garage.

Ian grabbed his bag from the passenger's seat and stepped out. He walked to the door to his cabin, pushed a button and watched the snow continue to fall until the garage door closed and blocked out the inclement weather he hadn't planned for.

He should've known this would happen. It was just one more thing in a string of screwups that had plagued his life the past few months. He knew that he should think of them as happy accidents, but he couldn't help but feel trapped by his circumstances. This weather was no exception.

Ian never came to the mountains in January or February. The weather was always too unpredictable this time of year. Living at the top of a mountain was luxurious and the view was incredible, but you could only benefit from it if you could get up there. He wouldn't be here now except that his fiancée, Missy, had insisted they take their engagement photos at the mountain house. Against his better judgment, he'd agreed.

Ian set his bag on the granite countertop and glanced out the bay window to the valley below him. It was a sea of white out there. At this rate, the few inches on the ground would easily reach half a foot or more. "No accumulation of note." He snorted after mimicking what the man on the news had said last night. Missy had left from Atlanta, so maybe the weather was better from the south, but likely it wasn't. He was pretty sure Missy wouldn't be able to make it up the mountain in her little Jaguar.

And the photographer... Who knew what kind of car he or she would be driving. If this storm had surprised him, it had probably surprised everyone.

Thank goodness he'd had the cabin stocked with supplies. Ian walked around the kitchen, opening the cabinets and the refrigerator to inspect the contents. There was enough to feed them for several days, as requested. His caretakers were a married couple who lived down the hill. They kept the grounds tidy and the cabin clean and well maintained. Before he made a trip to the house, he would give Rick and Patty a list of food and supplies and they would see to it that everything was there.

Sometimes Patty would even do a little extra to welcome Ian home. Today there was a bottle of champagne chilling in the refrigerator door and a pair of flutes sitting on the counter by a vase of fresh flowers. Neither had been on his list, so that was Patty's way of congratulating him and his new fiancée on their engagement.

She must have somehow missed the announcement that Missy was eight weeks pregnant. Missy had gushed about their newly forming family to anyone who would listen—from her two million Facebook fans to the journalist at some tabloid magazine. Ian didn't think there was a person left in the United States who didn't know about his personal business.

They would wed in March at a venue in Nashville that Missy had chosen. Ian had not been involved with the details. He had told himself, and Missy, that he was busy with work so she could plan whatever she liked. It was her big day, after all. The truth was that he was still coming to terms with all the new developments in his life. But he was hoping to turn that around.

He wanted this baby to be welcomed into a happy, loving family and he was willing to make the effort to turn that into a reality in the next seven months. It would take work on both their parts. Missy wasn't the easiest woman to be with. She was demanding, spoiled and used to people constantly telling her how wonderful she was.

They weren't a love match by any stretch of the imagination, but Ian was beginning to think love and the trappings that went with it were just a myth, anyway. Any marriage took work. Their situation might not be ideal, but she was going to have his baby and they were getting married.

He should make the most of a complicated situation. A romantic weekend together was just what they needed to stoke the fires. After all, plenty of men would love to marry Missy Kline. Her sultry voice and hard body had been a staple in Top 40 radio for the past few years. She was the star of Ian's record label.

At least she had been. Her most recent record hadn't done that well, but Missy wasn't worried. She had the wedding and baby to keep her relevant. Her manager had arranged to sell the exclusive story and pictures from their wedding to some magazine. They were working on making their upcoming ceremony into some television special. It was going to be invasive, and Ian hated the idea of the whole thing, but Missy was pretty business savvy. They couldn't pay for this kind of publicity. The day their engagement was announced and photos of her ring hit the gossip blogs, her latest song hit the top ten on iTunes. As her label, he couldn't complain. As her fiancé, he wasn't as thrilled.

This weekend they would take their engagement portraits and project the image of the happy power couple to the world. Then they would spend the next few days together trying to make it into a reality. A crackling fire, a stunning view, hot cocoa on the deck while snuggled under a blanket together... It would be a romantic music video come to life. He hoped.

Right now, he couldn't guarantee that any of it was going to happen. Missy had said the snow would be romantic. He had no doubt she'd changed her mind by now.

Frowning, Ian walked to the front door, opened it and stepped out onto the front porch. The snow was sticking in earnest now, piling on the grass and creating a solid blanket across the road. You couldn't even see the pavement. Or the layer of ice likely forming beneath it. In the South, it was rarely snow that was the problem. It was the ice that sent you skidding into ditches and sliding backward down hills.

As he watched the snow fall, a little white SUV rounded the corner and headed in his direction. His house was the last on the winding path, so once the car passed his closest neighbor he knew it had to be the photographer. If the photographer could make it from Nashville despite the weather, maybe Missy would make it in from Atlanta. At the very least, he knew the roads hadn't closed yet.

The SUV pulled up by the steps to the front porch. Ian pasted on his smile, readying himself for a day of Academy Award–winning acting. He took careful steps down the stacked stone stairs to greet the photographer and help bring in any equipment.

A woman in a tight pair of jeans and a fitted turtleneck with a fleece jacket over it got out. She was dressed for a January day in Nashville, not the mountains. The snow had obviously been a surprise for her, too. She had no heavy coat, no gloves and no scarf, and her red Converse sneakers would offer about as much traction on ice as baby oil.

At least she had a hat. Her long blond hair peeked out beneath the knitted cap pulled down over her head. She was wearing wide, dark sunglasses, so he could see very little of her face, but for some reason, she seemed familiar to him.

The woman slammed her car door shut and slipped off her sunglasses. "Hi, Ian."

In an instant, the face, the voice and the memories slammed together and socked him in the gut. It was Bree. Briana Harper. His freshman romance. The one who distracted him from his classes with her young, firm body and adventurous spirit. The one who dumped him at the lowest point in his life.

Ian swallowed the lump in his throat. "Bree? Wow. I had no idea you were, uh, that you would be…"

Bree winced and nodded. He could tell from the visible tension in her neck and shoulders that this was equally awkward for her. She was strung tight as a drum, and the familiarity of their past urged him to reach out and massage her neck the way he used to. But that was just nostalgia talking. He sincerely doubted touching Bree would help this situation.

"You didn't know I was coming?"

"No, I…left all the details to Missy. She didn't mention who the photographer would be."

"I knew that I should've said something," she began, "or given you some kind of warning in case you didn't know, but I'd hoped not to make a big deal of it. My business partners didn't know you and I were acquainted."

Acquainted. That was one word for it. Touched every inch of each other's bodies was another way to phrase it. Once the shock of her arrival faded, Ian let his curious gaze run over the rest of her once-familiar curves. There were more than he remembered, but they'd practically been kids then, still teenagers. Now she was a full-grown woman in a pair of jeans that looked painted-on.

"Is this going to be a problem for you?" she asked. "It's not for me. I intend to keep this very professional. Your fiancée doesn't even need to know we've met previously, if that's what you prefer."

"Yes, that's probably for the best." Although Missy claimed she had little competition, she was at the same time insanely jealous. She had made headlines for starting catfights in night clubs and industry parties. She'd snatched the extensions out of her supposed rival's hair for just *talking* to her ex-boyfriend at a promoted event in Las Vegas.

Ian hadn't given Missy any reason to be jealous, but he knew how easily that switch could flip in her. The last thing he needed was Missy throwing a fit about the photographer. They needed these pictures done and released to the magazine for the scheduled issue. They couldn't wait for someone else to come up here and replace Bree.

That is, if anyone else could even make it up the mountain. The snow was falling faster than ever now. "We'd better get your things inside," he suggested.

Bree nodded. When she turned to head toward the back of her car, her shoe skidded on the slick pavement. Her eyes widened and her arms shot out for something to steady her, but it was Ian's lightning-fast reflexes that saved her. He reached out, his arms encircling her waist and tugging her up and against his body.

Ian instantly knew he'd made a mistake. The whole length of her was pressed into him. The scent of her favorite lotion mingled with the baby shampoo she'd always used. The familiar combination rushed to his nose, bringing back flashes of hot nights in his dorm room and in the back of his car. His entire body tensed, the cold unable to dampen the sudden arousal that being near Bree had so easily caused.

Bree clung to him, her ivory cheeks flushed pink from the cold and a hint of embarrassment. Her baby-blue eyes met his for a moment and the connection between them snapped like a current flowing freely through a copper wire. It had always been like this. Even minutes after he'd had her, he'd want her again. Back then, if she wasn't in his arms, she was all he could think about.

He tore his gaze from hers, letting his eyes settle on the pink pucker of her mouth. That wasn't much better. Her lips had been the softest, most welcoming lips he'd ever encountered, before college or since. Kissing Bree had been one of the divine pleasures of his life. Losing that had been almost as hard as losing his music.

That thought brought him back to reality. Ian steadied her on her feet and then disentangled himself from her before he did something stupid like kiss her. Bree reached a hand out for the side mirror of her car, taking a solid step back from him.

"Thank you," she said, her cheeks now crimson. "That was really embarrassing."

"That was nothing," he said, more to himself than to her, but he followed it up. "Embarrassing would've been bruising your hind end on the driveway and getting your pants soaking wet and muddy."

"True," she said, looking around, apparently unwilling to meet his gaze again.

"Are your things in the trunk?" he asked.

"Yes." Bree perked up, seemingly happy to focus on her work again. With one hand on her car she stepped cautiously to the back and opened the hatch on her Honda. She slung a green backpack over her shoulder and then pulled out a few black bags and a tripod.

Ian took as much as he could from her and escorted her up the stairs into the cabin. He let her focus on setting up her equipment and turned to his phone as a distraction. Hopefully reading a couple emails would help dull the raging arousal that still pumped through his veins and clouded his mind.

He hadn't had a reaction to a woman like that since... He thought back and frowned. Since the last time he'd held Bree in his arms. Not even the belly-baring diva of his record label could match the need Bree built in him right now. He didn't want that to be the case—life would be so much easier if things were reversed—but there was no denying it.

Missy would have a glass-breaking fit if she knew.

Bree focused on setting up her equipment even though she knew it was a pointless exercise. An hour had gone by without any sign of his fiancée. If she didn't show up in the next half hour, the odds were that she wasn't coming. One glance out the window made it perfectly obvious that the drive in would be next to impossible.

She had barely made it up the mountainside herself. Her tires had spun a time or two, lodging her heart in her throat. But that was nothing, nothing compared to the collision she'd just had with Ian.

It had been nine years since they'd been together. She should be over him by now. Long over him. Yet, when she was pressed against the hard wall of his chest and

staring up into the dark green eyes she'd once lost herself in, the years apart seemed to vanish in an instant.
All the reasons she walked away, all the heartache and
the doubts, gone.

She thought he felt it, too. For a moment, she sensed
a connection between them. An instant of attraction and
longing had flickered in his eyes, a soft smile curling his
lips. And then he'd looked away. A hard glint had shone
in his eyes as he gently pushed her out of his arms.

And just as quickly, she'd realized she was a fool.

She hadn't been able to get to her equipment fast
enough. Bree needed the safety and security of her camera. It was like a barrier between her and the world.
As long as she only looked at Ian through the lens, she
would be okay.

At least that's what she told herself.

That didn't keep her from sneaking peeks of Ian
now as she worked. As much as she tried to focus, her
gaze would lift and she would take in a few seconds of
his broad shoulders clad in black cashmere. His strong
hands gripping his cell phone and typing madly at his
laptop computer. The firm curve of his rear, highlighted
by the custom fit of his gray wool pants…

Groaning, Bree focused her attention back on her
equipment. The work is what would get her through
this. It was just stupid, misplaced attraction mixed with
nostalgia and jealousy. It wasn't like things between
them had ended well. There were plenty of good reasons why they didn't work as a couple, and she had
broken up with him. No sense in pining for something
she had given up.

Not that it had been much to give up near the end.
During the last two months of their relationship, Ian
had completely changed as a person. Part of what had

initially attracted Bree to Ian was that he was as different from her father as a man could get.

Doug Harper was a certified workaholic. He was successful and driven, spending nearly every waking hour of his life managing his construction company. He'd helped build half of Nashville and had made a fortune doing it. Her mother had filled the empty hours by traveling around the world and spending her husband's earnings. That had left Bree alone at home with the housekeeper each night.

It had been a miserably lonely existence she didn't intend to repeat as an adult. She'd always told herself she wanted a man who came home at night. One who was more interested in living than working. Who would put more importance on family and love than money and business. A soulful musician fit the bill nicely.

Ian had been everything she wanted and he'd really had a shot of doing well with his music. Until he'd stopped playing music and dropped out of school to work at a record company. Suddenly, he'd always been working.

It seemed like overnight she had lost her musician and in his place stood a clone of her dad. It had broken her heart to watch it happen, but in the end, things had turned out for the best. Ian had become extremely successful and was marrying his pop star. She had a career she was proud of and hopefully would one day find the perfect person for her, too. The photo session shouldn't be awkward at all. At all.

So why did she have butterflies fluttering in her stomach?

Her thoughts were interrupted by Ian's voice. He was talking loudly to someone on the phone. He didn't sound happy, but she was relieved to hear it was the weather and Missy's tardiness that concerned him. For a moment, she'd thought he might ring up Natalie and demand another photographer. That would be so embarrassing. She couldn't go back to Nashville and face her friends after something like that.

"What?" Ian's sharp voice cut through the cabin, echoing in the large open space of the living room where she was unpacking. "Are you sure? No. No, of course I don't blame you. I want you and the baby to be safe. That's the most important thing. We can reschedule."

Bree froze, waiting to hear the rest of the story. She was thankful she'd opted to have Amelia book her a hotel room nearby. Making it back to Nashville in this weather was a dangerous prospect. She glanced out the large bay window that looked over the valley below. She couldn't see anything but white. No cars, no roads, no trees. Just white.

A loud curse followed by a hollow thunk startled her. She straightened up and turned back toward the kitchen. Ian blew through the archway a moment later, his jaw tight and the edges of his ears red with anger. He looked at Bree, about to speak, then he stopped himself. He shoved his hands into his pockets and took a deep breath. "She's not coming."

Bree had gathered that much. "What happened?"

"The roads are all closed unless you have snow chains and even then, some roads are impassable. Missy was coming from Atlanta. She made it as far as Maryville, but then they started sending cars back. There's no way to get here." He shook his head. "I should've waited to do this until we could drive up together."

Bree bit her lip, not quite sure what to say to that.

"I guess we can reschedule the session in Nashville, if that's easier."

He nodded, his gaze dropping to the polished wooden floors. "That's probably the best plan."

Bree nodded. There was a confusing pang of emotions in her stomach as she turned back to her equipment to pack up.

She was relieved that she didn't have to face his beautiful and successful fiancée today. She didn't really feel like snapping pictures while they posed together intimately and smiled at her camera. She'd dodged the bullet. When she got back to Nashville, she needed to confess the truth to Natalie. It was probably for the best that someone else handle their engagement portraits and maybe the wedding itself. There was being a professional and there was being a masochist. She recognized the difference now.

At the same time, she didn't want to leave. Walking out the door meant she might never see Ian again. When he'd held her outside, she'd felt a heat in her belly that hadn't burned that strongly in a long time. She wanted him to hold her again. To kiss her the way she hadn't been kissed in years.

She groaned inwardly and zipped her bag. Maybe she *was* a masochist. She was fantasizing about her ex. Her engaged, soon-to-be-a-daddy ex. The ex she'd broken up with because she couldn't take the sudden change in everything about him. Overnight, he'd gone from a music major to a record label toadie working eighty hours a week. Bree was certain none of that had changed. He ran a successful record label. Just because he took a weekend off to pose for engagement pictures didn't mean he was cured of his affliction.

Bree stood up and slung her camera bag over her

shoulder. She was about to grab another bag when she heard a loud knock at the door.

Ian looked at her and frowned before turning, walking over and opening the front door. An older man in a heavy jacket and cap was standing there.

Bree couldn't hear their conversation so she moved closer.

"I've been walking around to all the cabins in the subdivision while I can. Everything's shut down. During Superstorm Sandy we got a bunch of snow and it took a few days before they could get the roads cleared. They can't really start, though, until the snow stops falling. There's already ten inches on the ground and they're expecting upward of another fifteen or so before it's done. I've lived here twenty years and I haven't seen it fall this hard and fast."

"So we're stuck here, Rick?"

The older man nodded. "For a few days at least. That incline is too dangerous for the plows. Patty stocked the kitchen and I added half a cord of firewood to the pile. It should keep you until it's safe to head back to Nashville."

Bree heard the man's words, but part of her didn't quite process it at first. It wasn't until Ian closed the door and turned to look at her with an expression of pure agony that it clicked. It wasn't as simple as Missy not being able to get here. They also couldn't leave. They couldn't even get down the mountain so she could sleep in her reserved hotel room.

Bree immediately reached for the remote control and turned the television to the weather station. Hopefully the National Weather Service knew better than the caretaker. The map of the country finally came up and the woman in the nice suit pointed out the weather trouble spots. When she got to the Smoky Mountains, Bree gasped.

"...An unexpected barrage of snow in the area after two smaller storm cells merged into the newly dubbed Winter Storm Shana. Blizzard-like conditions are expected overnight with up to forty inches of snow. Roads are closed and the highway patrol is asking people to stay in their homes. Do not try to travel as emergency crews are having difficulty getting to distress calls."

At that, Bree's knees gave out and she plopped down into the armchair behind her. She was stuck here. With Ian. For an undetermined amount of time.

And Ian looked anything but pleased about it.

Two

Days. Days! Trapped in this house with Briana Harper. What, exactly, had he done to deserve this? He must have done something because if the past few months weren't karma coming back to bite him, he didn't know what it was.

Ian scowled at his phone as appointment change notice after appointment change notice came through. After finding out they were snowed in, he'd called his administrative assistant and asked her to clear his calendar through Tuesday, just in case. Each meeting on his packed schedule generated another email as it shifted ahead into an already overcrowded week.

On the plus side, he had his laptop and cell phone, and the cabin had DSL internet service, so the wheels of progress could still spin to a point. He might be stuck here with Bree, but it was a big house and he was a busy man. Certainly with three stories and twelve different rooms to choose from, they wouldn't have to cross paths very often.

He leaned to the side on his stool to peek into the living room. Bree was camped out there with her own computer and equipment. She'd been on the phone on and off, too. He'd tried not to listen, but it was hard not to. She'd called a woman named Natalie, then Amelia. The talk had been all about work and covering the weekend wedding festivities, but a part of him kept waiting to hear his own name.

Bree had mentioned that she'd kept their past together a secret, but surely now that she was trapped here with him, that information would be shared with her coworkers. In the scheme of things, it seemed noteworthy. Unless, of course, he was as distant a memory in her mind as his music was in his own. If that was the case, good for her. He hadn't been as lucky. Thoughts of Bree still plagued him, angered him. He'd be happier now if he could've forgotten about her. Sometimes the intricacies of his work would push the thoughts away, but a quiet moment always brought them screaming back into his head.

She'd called her mother and left a message so she wouldn't worry. One call she didn't make, however, was to a boyfriend or spouse. He'd thought for sure that a man would've met Bree's requirements by now. There were plenty of hopeful artists in the world for her to choose from. Or maybe she'd grown up and realized that it wasn't practical for an adult who needed to support a family. Not that he was bitter.

Finally, she'd called a lady named Julia at the Whitman Gallery and said she'd have to reschedule her final appointment before the showing.

Ian had been to the Whitman Gallery on several

occasions. They did a lot of special art showings and liked to feature local Nashville artists. Perhaps Bree was planning a show there. That would be a big step for her photography. Back in school she'd been big on nature and architectural photography. She took snapshots of people but almost never posed portraits. She'd told him once that she liked to capture genuine moments.

How things had changed! His engagement portraits were about as disingenuous as moments could come. But as he well understood, sometimes art had to give way to paying the bills, and wedding photography was a high-dollar business. The wedding industry as a whole was a racket. The paperwork Missy had brought home after she'd reserved the venue and put down the deposit nearly made him choke. The floral bill alone was running him nearly six figures.

Bree stood up and Ian quickly shifted his gaze back to his computer screen. He tried not to give her much notice as she came into the kitchen and opened the pantry doors. She pulled out a bag of coffee. "It's freezing in that big room. Do you mind if I make a pot of coffee? Will you drink some?"

"That's a good idea. I'll drink it." The thermos he'd demolished on the drive up here had burned off a long time ago.

Bree filled the coffeepot and went about setting the controls and adding grounds to the filter. "When it's cold like this, I need something warm to drink."

"I think we'll be drinking a lot of coffee, then."

"I noticed some decaffeinated herbal tea in the pantry, too. I'll probably switch to that in the evenings. Otherwise I'll be up all night."

Ian's brain instantly went to the nights he had kept her up without the assistance of caffeine. How many

times had he missed his 8:00 a.m. English lecture because he'd lost track of time in Bree's arms?

His eyes focused in on the curious expression on
Bree's face. "What?" he asked.

"I asked if you take cream and sugar," she said with
a smile.

"Yeah, two sugars. I like it sweet."

Bree got down the mugs and turned to him while
she waited for the coffee to finish brewing. "Still got a
sweet tooth, huh?"

He nodded, remembering all the junk he used to
eat back in college. Like any college student, he'd consumed his fair share of pizza and Chinese food, but
more often than not, he could be found with a candy
bar, a cookie or a can of soda in his hand. Sometimes a
combination of the three. "This machine runs on sugar
and caffeine most of the time. I have tried to scale back
a little. I have a one-candy-bar-a-day limit my assistant enforces by keeping snacks in a locked drawer in
her desk."

The warm scent of hazelnut coffee filled the air.
Bree turned to pour two cups and doctored them appropriately. She set a mug down next to his laptop and
crawled onto the barstool at the opposite side of the
kitchen island.

"I guess I always envisioned you marrying a pastry
chef. Or a chocolatier. I'm going to take a wild guess
and say that Missy doesn't bake."

"Lord, no." Ian chuckled. "I don't think Missy has so
much as turned on an oven in her entire life. She was
singing on mall tours at fourteen and was an opening
act for a world tour at seventeen. I signed her with Spin-
Trax when she was twenty. She knows how to work an
audience, but that's about it."

Bree took a sip of her coffee. "I suppose she doesn't eat that stuff, either."

"Missy doesn't eat much of anything."

Food was a constant point of contention in their relationship. Missy's personal trainer had convinced her that greens and fish were all she needed. Anything else and she'd blow up like a pop star has-been. When she'd announced her pregnancy, he'd expected her to add some foods back into her repertoire, but the opposite happened. Since she knew there were certain kinds of fish she couldn't eat, she'd gone fully vegetarian instead of taking the time to figure out what she could and couldn't have. She insisted that was why her belly was still as flat as it was on her last album cover. He wasn't sure how well she was going to take it when she hit the third trimester and even a strict diet wouldn't keep her from putting on a few pounds.

"I guess I'll never be a rock star, then. I like food too much," Bree said with a smile. "Of course, I've got the junk in the trunk to show for it."

One of Ian's eyebrows shot up. He'd tried not to look, but he'd noted Bree's trunk was nicely full. "I don't know what you're talking about," he said, trying to sound sincere without seeming too interested in her body. "You look great."

Bree smiled, a blush rising to her cheeks. She tucked a stray strand of blond hair behind her ears. "Thanks, but we both know this isn't the same body I had back in college."

"Thank goodness. I don't think I was skilled enough to handle curves that dangerous back in school."

Bree wrinkled her nose. "Were you always this big a flatterer?"

"I think so. I just did it with a song then. Now I have

to be more direct. I don't have time to beat around the bush."

Bree's bright blue gaze met his for a moment, and he felt the familiar heat rush through his veins once again. What was he doing flirting with Bree? He was engaged. He was going to be a father. He needed to focus on his relationship with Missy, not his past with Bree. How could he forget the fact that Bree had kicked him when he was down? That she had offered him the closest thing to a real relationship he'd ever had, then snatched it away?

Ian needed more space between them if he was going to get through the next few days. He couldn't decide if he wanted to kiss her or give her a piece of his mind. Neither was helpful. He remembered the feeling from school. She knew just how to push all his buttons and make him unsteady on his feet. Back then, it had brought on a rush of excitement. Now, it just frustrated him.

He had to give Missy credit in that department. He knew exactly where he stood with her: she was using him to salvage her career. There was no great love between them, at least when the cameras were off. It wasn't where he envisioned he would be with the mother of his child, but at least he understood the terms of the relationship. Bree was a wild card.

He looked back to his computer screen and closed his laptop. "I, uh, guess I'd better give you the tour so you can get settled in."

Bree slid down from the stool, carrying her mug with her as she followed him into the living room.

"This is the main floor. My bedroom is over there under the stairs." He gestured up to the loft overhead, then they headed up the steps. "You'll see there are two bedrooms and baths up here, and two more bedrooms and baths on the lower level. If I were you, I'd sleep up here, though. Because of the vaulted ceilings, upstairs stays a little warmer."

He led Bree back to the main level, past his bedroom door and down the staircase. At the bottom of the stairs was a spacious room with a big-screen television, a poker table, a pool table and a stone fireplace. "This is the game room. There's also a hot tub out that door on the deck."

He watched Bree roam around his vacation home, taking in every detail. She investigated both bedrooms, and then she looked out onto the deck. The direction of the snow was blowing such that it wasn't piling on the patio at all. That meant the front of the house would be waist-high in drifts by morning.

"This is really a beautiful place you have, Ian." Bree turned her back to the window and looked at him. "Do you get to spend much time here?"

Of course not. She had to have known the answer to that question before she asked it. It had been months since he'd last been here. Mid-September. Before his moment of weakness with Missy derailed his life. "Not as often as I'd like," he answered instead. "My mother and stepfather come up here from time to time. So does my stepbrother and his wife and kids."

"So your mom ended up marrying Ned?"

Ian's father had split nearly the moment he'd been conceived. When he was in high school, his mother had started a fairly serious relationship with Ned. Ned had one son of his own, a few years younger than Ian. "Yeah, they got engaged not long after you…" His voice trailed off. He was about to say "not long after you dumped me," but they were stuck here together. There wasn't much point in antagonizing one another, at least on the first day.

Bree's mouth tightened a bit, knowing what he'd been about to say. After a moment, she pasted back on her cheery smile. "How is everyone doing? I think about your family sometimes and wonder what they're up to."

Did that mean she thought about him, too? Ian knew he shouldn't care, but a part of him wondered. She'd certainly been on his mind over the years. Sometimes he was angry and bitter. Most times he just felt disappointed.

"Ned is getting ready to retire and my mother is trying to figure out what she'll do when she has to look at him all day. His son, Jay, and his wife just had their second child. They're all great. I actually haven't seen them in a while. Work has been pretty hectic."

Bree nodded and turned back toward the stairs. "You sound like my dad."

Ian noted the flat tone of displeasure in her voice. Bree and her father still had their issues, he could see. The man had been chained to his desk twenty hours a day when they were in college, and he blamed Mr. Harper in part for their relationship's demise. "How are your parents?" he asked.

Bree reached the top of the stairs and turned back to look at him. "Dad's recovering from bypass surgery after his second heart attack in five years."

Ian felt his own chest tighten in response. Bree had accused him of turning into a workhorse like her father. He tried not to work longer than eighteen-hour days, but that probably wasn't enough of a distinction in her eyes. Or the eyes of a cardiologist. "Is he okay?"

"Yes. He's too driven to die. But the doctors want him to scale back his hours and pass the running of the company on to his partner. That—" she laughed "—might actually kill him. That and the diet his doctors tried to put him on."

Ian nervously pulled at the suddenly tight collar of his sweater. He imagined the candy, coffee and liquor he consistently consumed was not on the doctor's recommended eating plan. "I'm glad he's doing okay. Is he back to work yet?"

"Yes," Bree said. "He returned to the office the day his doctor released him, although I suspect he'd been sneaking in some and checking his email from home. My mother divorced him last year, and he said it was hard for him to sit at home alone with the housekeeper. I find that kind of ironic considering that's how I'd spent most of my time. But his business is important to him. He's already sacrificed his family and his health for his job. It'd be a shame to lose his company, too. It's all he has left. You'd be wise to learn from his mistakes."

Bree had no idea why she'd said that last part, but the words left her mouth before she could stop them. It wasn't helpful. Or polite. Or any of her damned business. But a part of her just had to do it. If he was going to start a family, he should know what the price of his workaholic lifestyle would be. He should know what it would be like for his child.

Ian frowned at her and put his mug down on the side table. "What's that supposed to mean?"

Bree took a deep breath and shrugged. "You know what kind of hours you keep, Ian. They're probably worse than they were back in school when you forgot my birthday and left me alone night after night."

Ian widened his stance and crossed his arms over his

chest. "Are you still mad that I missed your birthday? I apologized twenty times."

"So did my dad, Ian. He apologized and bought me something expensive to make up for it, just to do it again. That's the point. You can work yourself to death, like my dad does. That's his choice. That's your choice now. But not when you have a family. Things are about to change for you. You can't work as hard as you do when you have a child at home who doesn't understand why you're never there."

"Since when do you know anything about me and what I do, Bree? You walked out of my life nine years ago."

That was an interesting way to look at how their relationship had ended. Her interpretation of the past was quite different. Bree planted her hands on her hips and prepared for battle. The minute she'd found out she was coming up here, she'd worried this moment might come. The presence of his fiancée would've kept the old feelings and hot tempers in check, but stuck alone? It was time to have the fight they'd never really had.

"How long did it take you to notice I was gone? A week? Two weeks?"

Ian clenched his jaw, fighting to hold back words he'd obviously suppressed all this time. "I noticed, Bree. I noticed that the woman I thought loved me just turned her back on me when I was at one of the lowest points in my life."

Bree scoffed at his cold assessment of her actions. "I didn't turn my back on you. You're the one who made this huge lifestyle shift and shut me out. Suddenly, you were all about working at that record company and you had no time for me anymore. You missed my birthday. You stood me up for that dance. You left me sitting alone at a restaurant waiting for you, twice. I did you a favor by easing your guilty conscience. You didn't have to feel bad about ignoring me if I was already gone."

"Thanks so much. I'm sure you were only thinking of me when you walked away. I made that huge 'lifestyle shift' because I was struggling to find my place in the world, Bree. You never realized how lucky you were. You were a talented photographer and you knew that your work could become a successful career for you. I had to face the ugly truth that my music wasn't good enough. *I* wasn't good enough. Do you know how much it hurt when my advisor told me that?"

Bree snuggled deeper into her fleece jacket, trying to disappear. She had assumed that time was hard on him, but he'd never talked about it. He had been like a steam locomotive that switched onto another track—he'd just kept on going. He'd started working at the record label, dropped out of school and charged ahead at full speed.

"How could I know anything, Ian, when you wouldn't talk to me about it? You never talked about anything important with me. You never shared your feelings. You saved it all for your songs. And when you lost that, you just clammed up and worked even harder."

She saw a touch of the anger ease out of his posture. His tense shoulders relaxed and his jaw unclenched. Ian shook his head sadly. "I never intended to shut you out, Bree. I just didn't know how to talk to you about it. I didn't know how to handle everything that was happening."

"I felt like I was losing you, little by little, like sand slipping through my fingers. At first I thought that job at the record label would help, but it just took over your life. You dropped out of school, moved off campus and wouldn't return my calls. What was left of the Ian I'd loved vanished. You were distracted, dismissive... I felt like I didn't matter to you anymore."

Ian ran his hand through the short, dark strands of his hair, the pain of that time in his life suddenly fresh in his eyes again. "Yeah," he admitted, "I threw myself into that job. But I was trying to find something I could do with my life. My dream of being a musician was dead, but at least working at that label let me keep my connection to the music industry.

"It's not an easy business, you know. Yeah, I worked long hours, but that's what they demanded. One of my professors got that gig for me. I couldn't disappoint him, especially when there was a line of other kids just waiting for me to screw up so they could take my place. So I fought for it. I put every ounce of energy that had once gone into my music into this work instead. And I succeeded. I climbed the ladder. I went out on my own and started my own label at twenty-five."

"You should be very proud of yourself."

Ian shrugged. "I guess. It wasn't an easy road, but I did it. It sure would've been a hell of a lot easier with you by my side."

"I know you think that, but it's probably not true. I would've been a distraction. You never would've gotten where you are now with a relationship making demands on your time. Besides," she said cheerfully, "things worked out for the best, right? You have your company, your fiancée, a baby on the way... Life turned out the way it was meant to."

Ian narrowed his green gaze and took a step toward her. "Do you honestly believe that? You haven't regretted the way things ended between us?"

Bree frowned and took a slight step backward, feeling her shoulder blades meet with one of the rustic wooden columns that supported the loft. "Of course I mean it. I mean, breakups happen and they're sometimes ugly, but you're happy with your life now, right?"

"If you believe what you read in the magazines, I guess so. I know I should be. I'm marrying one of the sexiest women on Earth. We're going to have a beautiful baby. My business is better than ever."

Bree's eyes focused on the slight downturn of his mouth as he spoke. He wasn't happy. Not at all. And she hated that. No matter what had happened between them, she wanted to see Ian happy. "So what's the problem?" she asked.

He took another step toward her, his height towering over her as he came nearer. "The problem?" A bitter chuckle escaped his lips. "Well, first, I'm not in love with Missy. Hell, I'm not even attracted to her. It's a long, sordid story I won't bore you with, but the punch line is that she's selfish and spoiled and doesn't give a damn about me unless there's a camera nearby. Second, she's the worst possible woman I could've chosen to start a family with. I'm already interviewing nannies because I know that's the person who's going to raise our child."

Ian leaned in, planting his palm on the polished wooden post over her head. "And to make matters worse, on top of all that, I find myself here. Trapped in a cabin with you. A woman who did love me once. One who would've made an excellent wife and mother. One who had the power to set my blood boiling with just a touch."

Bree drew in a ragged breath as Ian's hand brushed over her forehead and moved a strand of her hair from her face. Her entire body was tense, her stomach knotting tighter with every word he spoke.

"One who still has the power to make my entire body ache with the memory of making love to her," he whispered.

His gaze was focused on her lips as he spoke. He ran his fingers along her cheek and Bree's eyes instantly fluttered closed to savor the touch. The warm heat of his caress against her skin made her pulse pound harder than it had in a very long time. She took a deep breath and forced her eyes back open in time for his thumb to graze gently across her lips.

Was he about to kiss her? It would be wrong. So wrong. Yet, in that moment it was all she could think of. All she wanted.

"And I can't do a damn thing about it." He pulled away, taking several steps back as though her touch had nearly burned him.

Bree felt her knees weaken beneath her once he pulled away. It was as if he had yanked the rug out from under her. She righted herself and fidgeted, tugging anxiously at her pullover and tossing her hair over her shoulder.

What the hell was she thinking? She had very nearly melted into the arms of another woman's fiancée. She was their wedding photographer! Past or no past, that was all kinds of wrong. Natalie would kill her if she knew.

Bree took a deep breath and pulled herself together. Reacting to Ian didn't help either of them. "I'm sorry to hear your relationship is less than ideal," she said in her most formal, detached voice.

Ian's gaze ran over her face for a moment before he spoke. "Yeah. Me, too," he said, turning on his heel and disappearing into the other room.

Three

"Gretchen, I've made a big mistake."

Bree had made a quick getaway to her bedroom after her encounter with Ian. She'd needed some personal space to clear her head and purge her lungs of his scent. She'd hauled her bags up the stairs and selected the room with a wall of windows overlooking the valley below. The queen-size four-poster bed had a gray velvet brocade comforter and navy silk curtains to enclose the bed if she chose.

That wasn't a bad idea. The room was luxurious and spacious. Perhaps she should just wrap herself up in a silk cocoon and stay here until the snow melted. She could forage for food in the night while Ian slept and maybe squirrel away a box of crackers or something to keep up here. Maybe then they could stop antagonizing each other.

After closing the door, she'd grabbed her phone

and dialed one of her friends and business partners, Gretchen. Natalie would be horrified by the entire situation. Amelia would want to talk about Bree's feelings. But she just wanted to vent to someone who would listen, then tell her to put on her big-girl panties. That was Gretchen—their calligrapher, invitation and program designer and wedding day jack-of-all-trades.

"I hear you're snowed into a million-dollar mountain house. I really feel bad for you."

That was one way of looking at it, but it was getting harder and harder to remember that fact. The house *was* beautiful; every inch was filled with expensive furniture, detailed stone craftsmanship and state-of-the-art electronics. Her bedroom was nicer than some five-star hotels. "Did Amelia leave out the part where I'm stuck alone with the groom?"

"No, she mentioned that. Why does it matter? Is he creepy? Or a jerk?"

Bree hesitated. "No, he isn't creepy. But he is my... uh...*ex* from college."

"What?" Gretchen's sharp voice nearly climbed through the phone to smack her upside the head.

"Shh!" Bree insisted. She had no doubt that Gretchen was in the office and she didn't need her shouting to draw the others. "No one can know, okay? Especially not Natalie. She'll flip out."

"It sounds like *you're* flipping out. Is that what the thing Monday was about? Why you were so interested in the Missy Kline wedding?"

Bree frowned. "Maybe. It caught me off guard to find out he was getting married. And to her, of all people."

"So now you two are trapped together. What's going on that you're not telling me? You sound really wound up. The guy is getting married. And to Missy Kline! There shouldn't be an issue, even with your past together. Wait…you haven't tempted him away with your worn-out Converse and your messy ponytail, have you?"

"You hush," Bree snapped. She felt bad enough comparing herself to Missy; she didn't need Gretchen's help. "It's a proximity problem. We didn't exactly part well and being together after all this time…"

"Don't pick at the scabs, Bree."

"What is that supposed to mean?"

"I don't know what happened between you two, but considering I've known you for eight years and have never heard of you dating this guy, I figure you're picking at an old wound that should've healed a long time ago. You need to leave it alone or you'll reopen it. That's not the best idea when you're trapped in a house together. What good will it do to stir all that stuff up again, anyway?"

She was right. Nothing Bree said or did this weekend was going to change anything. When the snow melted, she would drive back to Nashville and resume her work. Ian would do the same. He might not be rushing home to reunite with the love of his life, but he would still go home to Missy and the baby. She had no doubt of that.

In college it had taken months to get Ian to open up to her about his family. He hadn't been much for talking about his personal life. It had been easier for him to communicate through song lyrics, but that had left no room for questions. That was probably how he'd liked it. But eventually, Bree had worn him down. He'd told her about how his father had bailed when his mother got pregnant. As he spoke she'd seen a haunting look of rejection in his eyes that Bree would never forget. Even though it really had nothing to do with him, he'd said he thought, deep inside, he wasn't good enough for his father to want to stay.

His college advisor echoing the same sentiment about Ian's musical abilities had been like a knife to his soft underbelly. He'd been defenseless to the attack and when it had come down to it, Ian had believed the man's words because he'd believed he wasn't good enough. Nothing Bree could say or do would've changed nearly twenty years of feeling inferior.

And nothing that happened this weekend would change the course Ian was on. He wouldn't do the same thing to his own child, even when the thought of being with Missy made him frustrated and desperate.

"It will do no good whatsoever," Bree answered Gretchen.

"Then steer your ship like you're in iceberg-filled waters. Stay diligent, keep your eyes open and avoid a collision. Eventually, you'll make it to port in one piece."

"Yeah," Bree said, her voice not sounding particularly confident.

Gretchen sighed. "Are you still attracted to him?"

The pointed question instantly flustered Bree. "What? Attracted? I mean, no, but then again, he's still… Yes," she spat out at last. "Because I'm an idiot."

She *was* still attracted to him. And she shouldn't be. It was so ridiculous. Her libido had flamed on like the Human Torch the minute she'd laid eyes on him again. The same libido that had been mostly ho-hum for the men she'd dated over the years. It was incredibly frustrating to find her body betraying her, especially over someone so unobtainable.

It was like her body remembered him. Nine years had done little to erase the claim he'd left on her. Just one touch and she was nearly putty in his hands again. Begging him to kiss her with pouty lips. Ignoring the fiancée unable to make it up the mountain…

"You're not an idiot. You just need to get laid."

Bree nearly choked. "Pardon?"

"You've just been working too hard with the gallery showing and all those post-Christmas engagement photo sessions. No time to play. And you haven't mentioned going on a date in forever. Maybe you should look into doing some online dating. It could help take the edge off."

That wasn't an entirely bad idea. Walking into Ian's house after months of celibacy had left her at a distinct disadvantage.

"Maybe you're right. If I keep my head down, I can make it through this." Even as she said the words, she didn't really believe them. She was a mess and it had only been… Bree looked down at her watch. Six hours. Only six hours with Ian had put her every nerve on edge. What would a few days do?

"Just remember," Gretchen said in a tone mocking the ever-proper Natalie, "keep it professional and keep it classy."

"Yeah." Bree snorted with contempt. "I'll do that. I'll call you later." She hung up and flopped back onto the bed. She closed her eyes, startling herself when the image of Ian hovering over her, midthrust, popped into her mind.

She shot up with a start. That settled it. She was going to lock herself in the bedroom. Bree pulled a book from her bag and set it by the bed. Investigating the large, marble, brass and glass tile bathroom, she decided that tonight she would crawl into her large whirlpool tub for a long, hot soak and read a book. She always lost herself in stories, so it would be an excellent distraction from Ian.

A disgruntled rumble sounded from Bree's belly.

So much for locking herself in the bedroom. She'd been up here a half hour and the rumblings of hunger pangs had already begun. She'd stopped for a quick bite on the road to follow up the granola bar she'd scarfed down before she left her apartment, but that had burned off. She could distract herself by unpacking her things and assembling her toiletries in the bathroom, but that would buy her minutes, not hours.

She needed to eat. And more important, she needed to desensitize herself to Ian. Perhaps the more they were together, the easier it would be. Either way, she couldn't ignore the inevitable. Eventually, Bree would have to go back downstairs and face him.

"Okay, I'm officially starving."

Ian looked up from his laptop to see Bree in the kitchen, searching the cabinets. He'd spent an hour or so staying as far as possible from her and focusing on work. After what had happened this afternoon, that seemed like the best idea. He wasn't entirely sure what had gotten into him. He'd been angry with Bree only moments before, and then suddenly, he had needed to touch her.

Relationships weren't exactly Ian's strong suit. He'd actually had very few that he'd even characterize as "relationships." He'd only been in love once, with Bree, and that whole thing had bitten him in the ass. From then on, dating had taken a backseat to work, and emotions usually had no role in the process. But he'd never been unfaithful to a woman. That just wasn't in his blood.

Besides, he was usually too busy with work to make one woman happy, much less two or three.

But here, now, for the first time, he was tempted. So tempted. How many times over the years had his thoughts strayed to Bree and where she was and what she was doing? And then to have her practically dropped into his lap by a weird twist of fate and weather...

Time had been good to Bree. He watched as she opened every single cabinet door, making thoughtful sounds as she moved around the gourmet, U-shaped kitchen. She was just as beautiful as he remembered, giving Missy a run for her money—and without three hours in the hair and makeup chairs to get there. She still had long honey-gold hair, which at some point today she'd pulled it into a messy knot at the back of her head. Her baby-blue eyes were just as bright. The freckles across her nose had faded, but she still had the same charming smile.

She looked almost exactly the way she had when she'd been his. It was hard for his brain and his body to recognize that was no longer the case. When his fingertips had brushed across her pink lips, they'd parted seductively, nearly begging him to kiss her. And he'd wanted to. Man, he'd wanted to.

Which was why he'd walked away. Why he had to stay away from Bree Harper.

Shaking away the unproductive thoughts, he looked down at his watch. It was after five. Food was probably a good idea. Bree had ended her quest at the refrigerator.

"Champagne, strawberries, spinach, brie...fancy stuff. Perfect if you're having acquaintances over for a wine soiree." Her blond head popped up over the door to look at him. "You don't happen to have makings for a cheeseburger tucked away in here, do you?"

He shook his head. "No, sorry. Missy doesn't eat red meat and she says that since she got pregnant, watching me eat it makes her ill."

Bree's lips twisted in thought. She eyeballed a loaf of sourdough bread on the counter and looked back inside the refrigerator. "How about grilled cheese and tomato soup?"

Ian's brow went up with curiosity. "Are you offering to cook us dinner?" The Bree he knew from college wasn't much of a culinary wizard. Of course, living in a dorm didn't exactly lend itself to cooking.

She shrugged, tossing a block of gruyere onto the counter. "One of us has to do it unless you have a personal chef hidden away somewhere."

"No." He chuckled. "I like to keep things more casual here, so I don't keep any staff."

"You have staff at home?" she asked while slicing the cheese on a wooden cutting board.

"I just have Winnie. She's… Well…I pretty much pay her to be my wife."

At that, the cutting stopped and Bree looked up. "Care to clarify that?"

"She takes care of everything at home so I can focus on work. Winnie cleans the house and does the grocery shopping. She cooks. She does my laundry and picks up my dry cleaning. Winnie pretty much does everything a wife who works in the home would do. I don't know how I'd survive without her."

Bree retrieved a skillet and a pot from the cabinet and put them on the blue flames of the stove. "Sounds handy."

"She is. I'm going to miss her when Missy moves in."

"Why is she leaving?"

That was a damn good question. "Missy is…particular. She has her own staff, which includes a housekeeper, a chef, a personal trainer and a personal assistant. She insisted there was no need to keep Winnie on when she moved in with her entourage. Once we add the nanny, that's just way too many people, although I hate to do it. I'm giving Winnie a huge severance package and I'm trying to find a new position for her."

Ian didn't mention that Winnie was relieved to be laid off. He got the distinct impression that she had no interest in looking after the pop princess. He didn't blame her. Missy was a handful.

He watched Bree at the stove. She had the tomato soup simmering and the sandwiches were turning perfectly golden and toasty in the skillet. He watched her give them an expert flip and then slip them onto a plate. The Gruyère cheese was oozing out the sides with crispy burned edges. She ladled the soup into big soup mugs and put them beside the sandwich.

"It may not be the gourmet meal a kitchen this grand calls for, but I can't think of anything else more perfect for a cold day in the mountains."

Ian picked up both plates and carried them into the dining room. "I agree. It smells great. I don't think I've had tomato soup since I was a kid."

"Really? Why was it in the pantry?"

He shrugged and put the plates down at two of the place settings near the fireplace. "It's probably left over from the last time my stepbrother came with the kids. They were here at Christmas."

They sat down together, the large stone hearth roaring with flames beside them and the picture window overlooking the valley opposite it. Ian found it unnerving that he couldn't see anything except the bare branches of the trees in his yard below. The snow was still falling as hard as before.

With a shake of his head, he took a bite of his sandwich and groaned aloud. It was probably the best grilled cheese sandwich he'd ever had. The gruyere reminded him of a *croque monsieur* he'd enjoyed so much in France. "This tastes wonderful."

"Thanks," she said before tentatively sipping a spoonful of the hot soup. "I'm not much of a cook. It'll probably be all downhill from here. Amelia won't even let me help in the kitchen when she's slammed."

"Who is Amelia?"

"One of my business partners at From This Moment. She's the caterer. You'd much rather be snowed in with her, I assure you. First-class cuisine all the way."

Ian sincerely doubted that. He'd take Bree's company and grilled cheese any day. "Does the wedding business take up all your time, or do you still have the opportunity to do the artistic photography you did back in school?"

A soft smile curled Bree's lips. "I do. This year, I've done a black-and-white series called 'The Other Side of Nashville.' I wanted to show the parts that most people don't think of. There's no country music, no cowboy boots. Just a collection of places I love and people who look less like Grand Ole Opry stars and more like middle America."

That was the Bree he remembered. The one who hated posed pictures. "Are you doing a show? I thought I heard you talking on the phone to someone at the Whitman Gallery earlier today."

"Yes." She brushed a stray stand of blond hair behind her ear. "It's the Sunday after next. I was supposed to have my last meeting with the curator tomorrow, but I obviously had to cancel. I'm going to meet with her as soon as I can get back to Nashville."

"Is this your first show at the Whitman Gallery?"

"It's my first show anywhere since college. And those hardly counted. I couldn't really focus on my art the first few years after we started From This Moment. Even though we all had our specialties, we had to roll up our sleeves and do everything from setting up chairs to sweeping floors. We couldn't afford to hire anyone to help us for a while. If I wasn't taking pictures, there were a million other things to be done. The last year or so, that changed. That's when I started my new collection."

Ian appreciated her work ethic. As fresh meat at the record studio, he'd sorted mail, emptied trash, fetched sparkling water for the singers...anything and everything they asked of him. That was just what you had to do.

"So tell me about the business you guys have going. Judging by what you've said and the estimate I received, you all are doing quite well now."

Bree chuckled. "Not all our weddings are on the same scale as yours. We have everything from week-long million-dollar extravaganzas to couples that elope in the garden with only their parents. Whatever a bride wants, we can make it happen."

"How did you start all this?"

"I met the others when I transferred to UT. During our senior year, while we were trying to think of what we wanted to do with our lives, one of us came up with the idea of a wedding facility. A friend had gotten engaged and complained that it was hard to find the right kind of venue that wasn't at a church or wasn't a tacky, in-and-out kind of chapel. We spent months putting together our grand plan and trying to round up investors."

"I can imagine it wasn't cheap to get off the ground."

"Oh, no. Even with some startup investments and money from my dad, we're mortgaged to our eyeballs. The initial costs were astronomical, but that's because you have to buy all the things you'll use repeatedly over the years like chairs and tables and stemware. Once you've got it, though, you've got it, and our expenses have gone down over time. Like I said, it took several years of hard work, but we've managed to make a profit every year. The facility itself will take a long time to pay off, but that's the nature of the business."

"Did you buy a place and renovate it?"

"No. We bought land and built everything exactly the way we wanted it. Natalie had a vision of how it should be laid out, and there was nothing even close on the market. Having a dad in the construction business certainly helped there. I probably saw him more that year than I did all the years before it."

Ian noticed the faint bitterness in her voice when she spoke. He knew her words earlier hadn't been solely intended to antagonize him. She'd meant them. She knew what it was like to be the child of a busy, driven man. He never wanted to do that to a child, which is why he'd deliberately not married or started a family. Missy getting pregnant was a mistake. Until he held his child in his arms, it would be hard to think otherwise.

"So...care to tell me what's going on with you and your pop star? It doesn't exactly sound like you two are living the fairy tale the magazines are reporting."

Ian sighed. "Can't we talk more about your photography? It's far less depressing."

Bree set down her spoon and crossed her arms over

her chest. "Come on, Ian. From what you told me earlier, seems like you need someone to talk to."

He popped the last of his sandwich into his mouth and stood up. "Wine first," he said, carrying his plate back into the kitchen. He opened the small wine chiller and perused the collection. A nice 1993 chardonnay ought to do the trick. "You want some?"

"Sure," she said, following him in and putting her dishes into the dishwasher. By the time she turned around, he'd poured two generous glasses and had one held out to her.

"So, Missy and I…" he began as he took a sip and walked into the living room. Ian settled into the large leather chair by the fireplace. "Were never really Missy and I. I signed her to my label three years ago. She was one of my first. She was on the brink of hitting it big and I signed her just in time. I've made a fortune on her, don't get me wrong, but she's been a handful from the start."

He paused to look at Bree. She was curled up in the chair on the other side of the hearth, listening intently. It was easy talking to her. It always had been. He didn't realize how much he'd missed that until this moment. He hadn't had any long, meaningful conversations that weren't about the business in quite a while.

"Her contract ended with this last album. It didn't do well. Her single barely cracked the Top 40. I wasn't happy with her, but she wasn't interested in anyone's opinion. It wasn't until I told her manager I wasn't going to renew her contract that she came around. Suddenly, she was all rainbows and sunshine."

That should've been his first clue. "One night she came in after hours. No one was there but me by then. It was nearly nine. She brought a sack of hand-rolled sushi and a bottle of premium sake. Missy said it was a peace offering. While we ate, she apologized for the way she'd acted. She was attentive, she was sweet and, before I knew it, the bottle of sake was empty and she was in my arms."

"She's smarter than she looks," Bree said.

"She definitely has a head for business, and I'm pretty sure our relationship is just business to her. She's certainly sold every moment to the press. To me, it was just a mistake I couldn't quite untangle myself from. I asked her over for dinner one night, fully intending to break it off. It had only been a few weeks, but it just wasn't working for me. She'd gone back to her old diva ways and nothing made up for that. The words were on the tip of my tongue when she told me she wanted to give me a present. Wrapped in a box with a shiny bow was the positive pregnancy test."

"Wow" was Bree's only response.

"I don't know how it happened. I'd taken every precaution. You remember how militant I was about using protection. But as Missy says, it must be meant to be. So we're getting married."

Bree studied him, the flickering flames of the fireplace dancing light and shadow across her face. "You know you don't have to marry her. You can still be a part of your child's life without marrying his or her mother."

At that, Ian vehemently shook his head. "You know that's not an option, Bree. Even if I financially supported our child and spent every moment I could with him or her, it wouldn't be the same. I want to do what's right for my child. I'm not going to be like my father and walk away from my responsibilities."

"How happy of a family will you be if you don't love his mother?"

Ian slammed back the rest of his wine. "Missy is having my child. We're getting married. End of story."

Four

"The internet isn't working."

Bree was admiring the wooden beams of the vaulted ceiling when Ian made his announcement. When the sun went down, she decided she was done worrying about work and their awkward circumstances. She was going to make the best of this situation. She'd gotten her camera out of her bag and started taking pictures of the beautiful details in the cabin. The craftsmanship that had gone into building this place was unbelievable. Ian had come a long, long way from the small, run-down apartment he'd grown up in.

She turned to find Ian checking the router and growling at it. From across the room she could see the lights weren't flashing like they should be. "It isn't? It was working a little while ago."

She watched him get up and walk over to the phone. He picked it up, listened for a moment and then put it down with a curse. "That's why. The phones are out. I have DSL out here."

"At least we still have our cell phones," Bree said brightly. "And power." With this storm and the low temperatures, power was critical. She was going to recommend they bring in some wood for the fireplace just in case the electricity went out in the night.

Ian eyed her, significantly less optimistic about their circumstances than she was. He walked back to his computer, grumbling the whole way. Bree returned to taking pictures of the hand-carved mantel around the fireplace and the painting she thought might be an actual Rembrandt mounted over it.

"You have got to be kidding me!" she heard him shout after a few seconds.

"What's the matter?"

He took a deep breath and tossed his phone onto the granite countertop. "I've got no bars, no data. Nothing. It hasn't rung for over an hour, but I thought maybe things were just quiet at the office tonight. I hope the storm didn't take out the cell tower. Is your phone working?"

Bree went to her purse and pulled out her phone. "No bars," she confirmed, looking at the grainy black and gray screen.

"What about data?"

She shook her head. "I have a dumb phone. Top of the line circa 2003. No games, no apps, no internet. I'm lucky it has a camera, although I wouldn't dare take a picture with it. The quality is terrible."

Ian looked at her as though she had sprouted a second head. "Are you serious?"

"Yes. I only have this one, really, because Natalie insisted she be able to get in touch with me for work. It's her old Motorola RAZR. I like it. It's pink."

"You have a flip phone with no internet. Hell, that thing doesn't even have a keypad, does it?"

"No. But that's okay because I don't text."

Ian ran his fingers through his hair. "What planet are you from? Seriously, I think you're the only person I know under the age of *seventy* that doesn't at least have a phone with the *ability* to get on the internet."

Bree frowned at him, defensively slipping her maligned phone back into her purse. "It might be able to get on, but I really don't care. I like the peace and quiet of unplugging. I like that people can't get ahold of me every second of every day. Sometimes, I actually turn my phone off and forget to turn it back on for days!"

She watched Ian's eyes widen in horror. "Listen," she explained, "when I go out into the woods to take pictures, I want to hear birds chirping and water rushing over the rocks, not some cheesy symphonic ringtone of an old eighties tune."

"If you had a cell phone from this decade, you could have ringtones made of real songs."

She shook her head. This wasn't the first time she'd fought this battle. As it was, Natalie made everyone in the office use laptops that detached from the keyboard as a tablet. Natalie was very plugged in, as were Gretchen and Amelia. Like most people were anymore. Bree was just resistant to the constant barrage of technology and information.

"No way. I've seen people and their phones these days. It's like an addiction. They've constantly got to check it, even if they're on a date or have all their friends with them. Who ignores their real friends to post stupid messages to people who are only their friends in cyberspace? *Everyone*, that's who. I work on computers because I have to, but I prefer to unplug and get away from all that when I can."

Ian crossed his arms over his chest and shook his head in bewilderment. "Well, congratulations. You've stumbled into the perfect storm. I, however, feel like my right arm has been amputated. How am I supposed to get anything done without phone or internet service?"

Bree set her camera down on the coffee table and walked over to him. He was tense and twitchy; the type A personality he'd evolved into over the years paced inside of him like a caged tiger. She put her hands on his shoulders to hold him still, ignoring the heat of his body radiating through his shirt. "Relax. Turn off your laptop. It's after nine on a weeknight. You don't need to be working, anyway."

She felt his muscles loosen under her fingertips. He looked around the house, seemingly at a loss. "What will I do, then?"

Bree shrugged. "Do whatever you like. Watch your big-screen television. Listen to music. Read a book. Talk to me. Play billiards downstairs. Enjoy this incredible home that you've obviously paid a fortune to own." He didn't seem convinced.

"Personally," she said, "I was thinking about taking a luxurious bubble bath in my garden tub and reading a paperback I picked up last week."

Ian chuckled. "Don't tell me, you don't have an e-reader, either!"

"No!" she said with a laugh, pulling her hands away from him. Touching him for too long was more comfortable than it should have been. When he smiled down at her, it would've been easy to lean in and rest her head on his chest. Not an option. Why did she have to keep reminding herself that *she* had broken up with *him*? And for a good reason. A reason that was still very applicable, given how sore he was over losing internet access.

"Maybe I'm just old-fashioned, but I like the smell of the pages and the ink. I like the weight of a book in my hands and the texture of the paper between my fingertips."

"You're a Luddite."

"I have a digital camera!" she countered. She'd only had it three months and she still preferred her old-school SLR camera, but she was getting used to it. She liked being able to take as many shots as she wanted and not worry about wasting the expensive, and getting hard to find, film. "Trust me, that's progress for me."

The banter between them seemed pointless, but it had served a purpose. Ian had finally relaxed a little. Making fun of her was apparently a soothing activity for him. Well, whatever helped them pass the time the next few days. If he was mocking her, maybe she wouldn't notice the full lips doing it or the way his emerald-green eyes watched her when he thought she wasn't looking.

"You're just going to read your paperback book and leave me here twiddling my thumbs?"

He looked pretty pathetic, like a lonely child. She supposed the book could wait. "Do you have games or something? Cards, maybe?"

Ian shrugged. "I have no idea. My family might have brought some games up here. I'm usually here alone, so I don't play games aside from the ones on my iPad."

Bree walked over to the closet by the stairs. "Let's see what we can find. A rowdy game of Scrabble or Sorry! could help pass the time." She opened the door and flipped on the light, which illuminated a stash of cleaning supplies and a bookshelf filled with assorted games, puzzles and crafts. "Yep, here we go. You've got Monopoly, Life, Clue, Sorry!, Scrabble and a couple decks of cards."

"Pick whatever you want. I really don't care."

Bree reached out for one of the games and noticed a familiar shape sticking out from behind the shelf. A dusty, old acoustic guitar was propped in the corner. Bypassing the games she'd come in search of, she reached down and picked it up.

After pulling the strap over her shoulder, she made a poor attempt at strumming it. "What have we here?"

"Did you—?" He stopped speaking when he saw her come out of the closet with the guitar. "That's not Scrabble," he noted.

"Nope, but I found something better," she said in a singsong voice, continuing to fumble at the strings. She had zero musical ability. She had an eye for beauty, not an ear for it. That didn't mean she didn't appreciate it in others. Few things had ever been as soothing to her as the sound of Ian strumming his guitar and singing to her.

Wouldn't it be wonderful if she could get him to play for her again? It would be amazing to hear him after all these years. Then, maybe, for a short time, she could be reminded of the man he'd been *before*. She missed that Ian.

Ian took a few steps back from her as she came closer with it. Apparently, the idea was not as intriguing to him. "I thought I threw that out," he noted with a look of distaste.

"I don't know much about musical instruments," Bree said, "but I can tell this is a high-quality guitar. Don't you dare throw it out."

"It's old. The same one I had in college, actually."

"That's like saying a Stradivarius is an old violin so it should be thrown away. Is it really the same one you used to play at the Coffee Bean?"

"Yes. Flip it over, you'll see."

Bree lifted it off her shoulder to examine the back. There, carved ever so carefully was "IL & BH Forever." It was the same guitar. She ran her fingers over it, the sight of the familiar carving forming a lump in her throat. She remembered the night he'd put that there with his pocketknife. The memory and the emotions hit her all at once. "That was the night…" she said, her voice drifting off.

"I told you I loved you for the first time." A faint smile curved his lips as he remembered it, too. "We sat on the lawn outside the quad and looked up at the stars while I played the new song I wrote for you."

Bree felt the prickle of tears in her eyes. The blanket under the stars, the sweet melody of a love song, the strong arms of a man who loved her… When he'd carved their initials into the guitar, it had felt as if they were sealing their future together. It was the most romantic night of her life. Nothing before or since had ever come close to that moment. How many women had had a man write a song for them? It was a sentimental, romantic tune that had made her eighteen-year-old heart thump like a jackhammer in her chest when she'd heard it.

"'I'll Love You Forever, And Then Some,'" she said. Ian had been such a talented artist. He was gifted with an ear for melody and a perfect lyric. His stuff was better than most of what she heard on the radio these days. "I might be partial to it, but I always thought that was your best song."

Ian nodded. "I thought it was, too." He reached out

and took the guitar from her. Her breath stilled in her lungs for a moment, thinking he might play a song or two for old time's sake. She longed to see him play again, to sing the way he used to. To feel that flutter of excitement and desire curling in her belly. Ian was a handsome man, but she was never as attracted to him as she was when he played.

Instead, he held it by the neck at a distance, as though it might contaminate him if it got too close. "It's a shame my advisor disagreed."

He brushed past her to the closet and unceremoniously flung the guitar back inside. With a slam of the door, he turned back to her with a pained expression lining his brow. "But he was right," he said. "After years in the music industry, I know better now. He wasn't being cruel—he was being kind. Someone had to tell me I wasn't good enough."

At that, Ian turned and disappeared into his bedroom, shutting the door behind him.

With a disappointed sigh, Bree made her way to the staircase. Maybe it was just as well. She couldn't afford to lose control and act on her building need for Ian. With that guitar in the closet, her desire could also stay firmly locked away.

Damn that stupid guitar.

What the hell was it doing here, anyway? Ian paced around his bedroom, irritation surging through his veins. He'd paid movers to bring furniture and some personal items to the house after it had been built. They must have grabbed it by mistake. He certainly hadn't brought it, and his mother knew better than to bring a musical instrument into the house.

How many times had he been up here and never

known it was hidden away? And of all the people to find it—it had to be Bree!

With a sigh, he flopped down onto his bed and dropped his head into his hands. That stupid guitar had flooded his brain with memories he didn't need right now. Good ones of loving Bree and bad ones about losing his musical career. Either way, he had no use for the thoughts and images that haunted him. He was going after that guitar with an ax first thing in the morning. It would make good kindling for the fire.

Not long after he went into his room, he heard the water running upstairs. He assumed that it was Bree taking the bath she'd mentioned. That didn't help matters. The sound brought to mind unwelcome images of her creamy, naked skin, slick with soap and glistening in the steaming, hot water.

Maybe he could break the guitar by repeatedly bashing it against his skull until every thought about Bree was driven from his mind.

He loathed himself in that moment. Ian wasn't his own biggest fan to begin with, but he'd really taken the crappy cake this time. He was not allowed to be attracted to Bree. He was engaged to Missy. He was determined to be a good father, better than his own. That meant marrying the mother of his child and being a part of his life, whether it made him happy or not. He knew what it was like to not feel important enough to matter. Ian might not be happy about the turn his life had taken, but he would never, ever let his child feel that way. His son or daughter would feel loved, special, important... He would see to that.

Being attracted to someone else while the future mother of his child was miles away was an epically bad start.

Ian needed a distraction. He picked up a random book from his bookshelf and forced himself to read it for nearly an hour. By then, he thought perhaps the phone gods had smiled on his pathetic situation and brought back his connection to the world. As he slipped from his room, the house was quiet. Bree was probably asleep by now. He ventured back out into the living room and found that all the lights were off on the ground floor. Only the small light over the kitchen sink was burning. His phone was on the counter where he'd left it. There was still no connection, making it just as useless as before, except now it also needed charging. He dug the cord out of his bag and plugged it in by the coffeepot.

He picked up the house phone. No dial tone.

With a sigh, he went back into the living room and flopped down on the couch. It was nearly midnight now, but he couldn't sleep. His brain was spinning and there was nothing to soothe it.

When he was younger, the music had helped. The doctors had diagnosed him with a hyperactivity disorder when he was a child, but his mother had refused the medicine. She had been determined to find a way for him to channel his energy. He'd played soccer for a while, but the real change had come with a chance encounter at a pawn shop.

He and his mother had gone there to pay off a debt she had against her mother's wedding ring. They'd needed the money for rent. While they were there, a guitar had caught Ian's eye. It had been way more expensive than he could afford. He had been only thirteen at the time. The man who ran the shop had offered to trade Ian the guitar for help on the weekends cleaning up the stockroom. He'd snapped up the opportunity and continued to work there after it was paid off to fund guitar lessons.

Music had changed Ian's life. It had given him focus. It had helped him in school. Writing songs had come easier to him than any homework assignment. When he'd gotten to high school, he had joined the jazz ensemble. Some of the happiest days of his teen years had been spent holding the very same guitar that was in the closet right now.

Ian felt a pang of guilt for handling it the way he had. It wasn't the guitar's fault that the person playing it wasn't any good. He sprung up from the couch, walked to the closet and turned on the light. The guitar was haphazardly lying on the ground, a flutter of loose Monopoly money on top of it. Apparently, he'd knocked the game off the shelf when he'd flung the guitar inside.

Reaching down, he picked up the instrument and carried it back into the living room. A quick inspection proved he hadn't damaged it, thankfully. Ian sat down on the couch and cradled the weight of the guitar in his lap. It seemed like forever since he'd touched a guitar. He'd quit his music cold turkey. If he didn't have what it took to succeed, he hadn't wanted to waste another minute of his life on it.

Now his fingers itched to brush the strings. What could it hurt? Bree was asleep upstairs. If he played quietly enough, just one song to soothe his curiosity, no one needed to know.

He turned the guitar and gripped it. The first few notes were off, so he took a moment to adjust and tune it. His first solid chord sent a shiver down his spine. It was like his soul had reconnected with its true passion again. He began a quiet, mellow song—one of his coffee-shop favorites—to test himself. He wasn't as rusty as he thought he'd be. The music flowed smoothly, the chord changes, second nature.

When that song was done, he tried another, this time singing along. That song seemed to fly by. He remembered how easily the time would pass when he played. The same happened with his work now; he lost himself in it. This was a lot more enjoyable, though.

With a happy sigh, he looked down at the guitar and the carving on the back. One last song.

He started playing his acoustic cover of "Hello" by Lionel Richie. He remembered that he'd serenaded Bree in the coffee shop with that song the first night they'd met. He'd noticed her earlier watching him play and he'd found himself looking up at her again and again. She had looked beautiful and so intense in the way she studied him. When he'd gotten to this song in his set, he'd stood up, walked through the shop and sang the last chorus directly to her. Then he'd asked her out. When she accepted, the audience cheered.

Playing this wasn't the smartest thing to do considering he was trapped in this house with her, but he was going to finish what he started. Closing his eyes, he let the music flow from him. He easily connected with the emotion of the song and the memory of the first moment he'd laid eyes on Bree. As he reached the last few notes, sadness washed over him.

It was done. Both his music and his time with Bree. The guitar and the memories needed to go back into the closet.

"That was always one of my favorites."

Ian leaped off the couch, his heart shooting into his throat. He spun to find Bree at the bottom of the stairs. How long had she been listening? He felt an uncharacteristic flush of embarrassment rise to his face.

"I'm sorry," he said. "Did I wake you up?"

"No. I couldn't sleep so I was reading my book. I was coming downstairs for a drink when I heard the music. I didn't dare interrupt you."

Ian shrugged. "You should have. I let it go on too long."

Bree walked across the room to stand beside him. Her long blond hair was pulled up into a messy knot on the top of her head. She was wearing a pair of flannel pajama pants and a long-sleeved shirt. On anyone else, he imagined it would be like a splash of cold water on his libido, but on Bree it was anything but.

The plaid pants rode low on her hips, showing a scant inch of skin when she moved and her shirt rode up. She wasn't wearing a bra. He could make out the full, round curves of her breasts and the tantalizing result the cold air had on them. He had to shift the guitar down a touch to save himself additional embarrassment.

"Play another one. Play *my* song."

Ian stiffened. He wasn't sure he could do that. Or that he should. There were way too many emotions wrapped up in the song he'd written for her. "I don't know, Bree."

"Please." She took his hand and led him back to the couch. Her wide blue eyes pleaded with him in a way he knew he wouldn't be able to resist.

He followed her because he couldn't help himself. Her touch was magnetic, the tingling draw of positive and negative coming together and refusing to part. Before he knew it, he was back on the couch again and Bree was beside him, waiting with nervous anticipation to hear him play her song.

There was no getting out of it without being rude. No matter what, he didn't want to be unnecessarily mean to Bree. He could play the song. It was just one song. It didn't have to mean anything. He just had to make sure he focused one hundred percent on the guitar and the song and not on her. Sitting this close, he could smell the scented lotion she'd always put on before bed. Touching her hand was enough for him to know how smooth and soft every inch of her skin would be.

Closing his eyes to block out those thoughts, he concentrated on the music and the lyrics he'd gone so long without bringing to life. About halfway through, he opened his eyes again. It was so quiet in the room he wondered for a moment if she had left.

But she hadn't. She was there, listening intently with glassy tears shimmering in her pale blue eyes.

Without meaning to, he stopped playing. The sight of her tears had made his chest suddenly too tight to keep singing. "Are you okay? I—"

In an instant, Bree leaned in and kissed him. Her lips met his with the force and emotion that only nine years apart could create. Ian was startled by the sudden attack, but he couldn't pull away from it. Right or wrong, he still wanted Bree. His brain and his body refused to get on the same page when she was touching him.

It was a mistake, but he was going to enjoy every moment while he could. Bree's kisses were an experience to cherish. Her lips were soft and tasted like the peppermint tea she'd drank earlier. She made soft noises against his mouth, her hands caressing the stubble of his jaw. It aroused a primal instinct deep inside Ian.

The surge of need shot down his spine. Every nerve ending awakened with a desire he hadn't felt in a really long time. He cursed the guitar between them. He wanted to wrap his arms around her and pull her tight to his body until those full, perky breasts crushed against his chest.

"Bree," he whispered in a half groan against her lips.

The sudden sound seemed to snap her out of the haze. In a flash, Bree had flattened her back against the other side of the couch. Her wide eyes flickered with emotions that Ian couldn't interpret. Then her hand flew to her mouth and smothered an *"ohmygod"* before she leaped to her feet and ran up the stairs to her room.

Five

Normally, Ian popped out of bed at six in the morning. It didn't matter if he was at the office or working on his laptop into the wee hours of the morning. Every day his eyes would open to a room dimly lit by early-morning sun, and he would immediately check his phone.

This morning, Ian rolled over and reached for the phone, but it was nowhere to be found. Then he remembered. It was charging in the kitchen. Opening his eyes, he was surprised to see how bright the light was coming in the windows. It must be the sun reflecting off all that snow.

Ian sat up and looked at the clock on the bedside stand. It was nine-fifty in the morning. He rubbed his eyes, expecting the digits to shift, but they remained stubbornly in place. He'd slept until nearly ten.

He threw back the blankets and slipped out of the bed. The wooden floors were cold against his bare feet, but he didn't care. He needed to get his phone.

His phone without service.

His fuzzy morning brain finally put the pieces together. He could go out there and check it, but considering he was wearing only boxer shorts, that was probably a bad idea. At this late morning hour, Bree was no doubt awake and roaming around the house. Last night, she had fled the room like her hair was on fire. Parading around half-naked wouldn't make matters better for either of them.

A shower, he decided. That way he could go out dressed and presentable, and his phone would have thirty minutes or so more time to get back to functionality.

Climbing into the large tile enclosure, he turned the knobs that activated the multiple showerheads and body sprays. The scalding-hot shower felt wonderful as it pummeled his body from all angles. Ian was warm-blooded, always flinging back the blankets and going without a coat, but even he was getting chilly with all this snow. He dried off quickly and slipped into casual clothes. A pair of jeans and a sweater seemed appropriate attire for being snowed in at a mountain cabin.

He laced up his boots so he could go outside later. He needed to bring in more firewood and, if he could, shovel a path to the road.

Finally, he emerged from his room and found the house still and quiet. A pot of coffee had been brewed, so he poured a cup and glanced out the window over the sink.

The snow had stopped and the sun was out. That wasn't saying much. The massive piles of white fluff were hip high in some places. He couldn't tell his front porch from his driveway from the road. It was just white in every direction. Maybe shoveling was a pointless venture.

A soft chirp distracted him from his investigation. He ignored it for a moment, then realized the significance of the sound. It was his cell phone. It was working!

Lunging across the countertop, he snatched up his phone and hit the button to activate the screen. Five beautiful bars and 4G data. He had never been quite so happy to see these old friends.

He had missed a lot. His screen was crowded with pop-ups about missed calls and texts and a hundred unread emails. That was more than even he had been expecting. What the hell happened last night?

A noise from behind him in the dining room forced Ian to look up from his phone. Bree was coming in through the glass door that led out to the covered, wrap-around porch. She was bundled up in a quilted blue coat that must have been in her luggage. It was almost the same color as her eyes. Her long blond hair was in a thick braid over her shoulder, a knit cap tugged over her head. She was red-cheeked from the cold but smiling. She had her camera with her. She must have gone outside to take pictures.

"You're up," she noted. "I was beginning to worry that old guitar had sucked out your soul. That, or I'd made such an ass of myself last night, you were afraid to come out of your room for fear I might throw myself at you."

"Neither," he said. Truthfully, if he thought she would throw herself at him again, he'd have slept on the couch to catch her the minute she woke up. But they were both adults and knew the kiss they'd shared last night was a mistake. He wouldn't even have mentioned it happened if she hadn't. Ian didn't want things to be more uncomfortable than they already were.

"I guess without my phone chirping and beeping at me, I slept later than usual. It's working again," he added cheerfully, holding it up with a triumphant smile.

"Oh, good. The balance is restored to the Force."

Ian chuckled. "I think so. But it seems that everything went crazy while it was down. I have twenty-five missed calls, ten voice mail messages, fifteen missed texts and a hundred emails."

Bree set her camera on the granite bar and walked over to make herself a cup of coffee. "You're more important than I gave you credit for."

"Not really. Most of it is from Missy. That's weird. She's not the best at keeping in touch. Besides, she knows I'm stuck up here in bad weather. I'm not sure what she expects me to do about whatever is happening."

"You don't think she found out you're up here with me, do you?"

Ian shook his head. "No. She wouldn't know who you were, anyway."

Bree pouted. "You mean you've never told her about your college romance?"

He shrugged. "We don't really talk about me."

Bree's eyes widened at him for a moment, but she didn't respond. She just turned back to sweetening her coffee. Ian was relieved. He didn't really want to explore that topic so early today.

Thumbing through his screen, he saw a phone message from his label's talent manager, Keith. He would listen to that first. Business before Missy's drama.

"Ian! Call me the instant you get this message. I've got press crawling all over the studio. I had to hire some private security to patrol the parking lot. This mess has totally blown up. I wish to God you weren't trapped in the mountains."

Ian's heart started racing. His fingers fumbled for a moment as he tried to hit the buttons to call Keith back, but he finally connected and it starting ringing.

"Is everything okay?" Bree looked concerned.

He shook his head. "I don't know yet." Keith finally answered. "Keith! What the hell is going on? My phone has been out since yesterday afternoon so I've been out of touch."

There was a painfully long silence. Ian expected Keith to start spilling the information, so the quiet was even more disconcerting. "Have you spoken to anyone?" Keith finally asked.

"No. You're the first person I called. I have a million messages, though."

"Oh, Christ." Keith sighed on the phone.

"What is it? Is everything okay?"

In an instant, the worst possible scenario popped into his mind. The frantic calls and texts from Missy. The press swarming the studio. Keith's dismayed tone. Something had happened to the baby. The dull ache of dread pooled in his stomach and tears welled up in his eyes. Not that. Anything but that. He could barely form the words to ask. "Is the baby okay, Keith?"

Keith groaned. "Ian, I swear to you that no one is dead or injured. Your mom, your stepdad, everyone is okay. But there's something I've got to tell you, man. Are you sitting down?"

"Yes," Ian lied. He took bad news better standing up so he could pace across the floor and burn off all the nervous energy. At the very least he knew his family was okay. The baby was okay. He could deal with anything else.

"A story about Missy hit the tabloids yesterday. It's all over the place—television, magazines, blogs. Apparently a woman in Nashville has come forward claiming that she sold Missy a positive pregnancy test on Craigslist."

With only a few sips of coffee under his belt, it took a moment for Ian to process what his friend was telling him. Missy had bought a used pregnancy test. A *positive* one. That meant...

"There is no baby, Ian. There never was."

"So she's not really pregnant? It was all just a ruse to..." To what? Mess with his head? Trick him into marrying her? Keep him from dropping her from his label?

Yes, yes and yes.

He'd always known Missy was ruthless when it came to getting what she wanted. But he'd never thought even someone like Missy would stoop *that* low.

"That's what they're saying. The evidence is pretty damning. The woman who sold it to Missy was no fool. When she realized who she was talking to, she knew there was a bigger payday than just the hundred bucks she'd make selling the test. She kept screenshots of her email conversations with Missy and took a photo of her Jaguar leaving the parking lot where they met. Personalized plates and all. It's all online if you want to look."

Ian wished he had taken Keith's advice and sat down. He stumbled over to one of the tall bar stools and leaned against it with one hip to steady himself. Missy wasn't pregnant. *Not pregnant.* Could it really be true? It sounded like a pretty credible case against his fiancée, but Ian wouldn't let himself completely believe the story until he spoke with Missy directly. More convincing lies had been printed in the tabloids.

Yet, it *felt* true.

He'd been meticulous in protecting himself over the years. There hadn't been so much as a late period scare with a girl he'd dated since he lost his virginity. He never wanted to make the same mistake his father had made by creating a child he had no interest in. If and when he had a child, he was going to be dedicated to it, no matter what.

Missy showing up with that pregnancy test had thrown him for a loop, but he'd recovered. He'd tried to make the best of it and stay involved, but Missy seemed determined to keep the baby stuff at arm's length from him. She had refused to let him come to the doctor's appointment with her. He'd wanted to hear the heartbeat, but she'd said it was too early. When she hadn't come home with one of those grainy pictures, she'd told him the sonogram machine was broken. Her flat belly hadn't budged. No morning sickness. No sign whatsoever that she was having his child.

She'd lied to him about the whole thing. He felt sick. Lightheaded. Foolish. But the strongest feeling sweeping over him was that of utter and complete relief. A moment ago, he'd been devastated that he might have lost his unborn child. Now, the child had never existed, was nothing but the manipulative imaginings of its would-be mother. He felt a bubble of hysterical laughter rising in his chest that he absolutely couldn't let out. Keith and Bree would confuse the sound for one of happiness, and that wasn't an accurate description of the maelstrom swirling inside him.

"Ian? Are you okay?" Keith's voice had more concern in it than Ian had ever heard before.

Ian cleared his throat, swallowing the emotions inside of him before his manager panicked. "Yeah. Thanks for telling me, Keith. It's better I heard it from you."

"What shall I do about the reporters?"

"Tell them that SpinTrax does not comment on the personal lives of their artists or employees. Then send them to Missy's house."

Bree was afraid to speak. Afraid to move. She was trapped in the kitchen, bearing witness to an uncomfortable situation she had no business in. She had only heard one side of the phone conversation, but that was enough. Judging by Ian's suddenly pale complexion and unsteadiness, she knew whatever Keith told him was bad.

She waited patiently for Ian to turn off his phone so she could see if he needed anything. In a moment like this, there wasn't much she could do, but she knew enough to offer. It was the sentiment that was important. If he preferred to be alone, she would go downstairs to give him some privacy. There, she could turn on the television so she couldn't hear his voice upstairs.

"Ian?"

He looked up from the phone. He seemed shaken but, at the same time, eerily calm. She knew from experience that wasn't good. He was thinking. Processing. Preparing. Fighting with Ian had always been frustrating for her because the majority of the fight seemed to go on silently in his head. She would say something and just sit back and watch the wheels turn in his mind while, outwardly, it appeared he was ignoring her. Eventually, she would just stomp away and he would throw himself into his music. Or his work. This wasn't a problem he could ignore, though.

"Yes?" he answered softly.

"Can I do anything? Get you anything?"

"No," he said with a slow shake of his head. It made Bree wonder if maybe he was in shock over the whole thing. She supposed that whether the baby was ever real or not, it had been real to him. He was still losing the idea of a child and the future he was planning with it.

"I need to call Missy here in a minute. You might not…" His voice trailed off.

Bree nodded. She wouldn't want anyone else around when she had a hard conversation like that, either. "I'll give you your privacy. Let me know if you need me." Bree reached out and put her hand over his. She gave him a reassuring squeeze and a weak smile before heading downstairs.

When she reached the lower level of the cabin, she walked over to the leather couch and scooped up the remote. She put the television on a loud action movie with lots of gunfire and explosions. But even that couldn't muffle everything.

The calm from a moment before was gone. She couldn't make out exactly what he was saying, but Ian was yelling. Bree turned up the volume and wished she had packed some earplugs in her bag. She considered taking a shower. Or a walk. Or crawling under some blankets and covering her head with a pillow.

She felt awful for Ian. She knew he wasn't happy, but he had been making the best of things for the child's sake. He had always told her how important being a good father was to him. In her young, girlish fantasies, she'd imagined what Ian would be like with their children. She'd thought he would be a hands-on dad. She'd had fantasies of him singing them to sleep with lullabies he wrote especially for them.

To think that Missy had taken that loyalty and dedication in Ian and used it against him… It made Bree feel sick.

Despite the fact that Bree had broken up with Ian in college, she'd never wanted to hurt him. She'd tried to help him, but when that had failed, she had to err on the side of self-preservation. She couldn't have sat back and watched his downward spiral any longer. Not when she'd loved him so much.

And she still cared about him now. She didn't want that to be the case, but seeing Ian again had brought all those old feelings to the surface. In only a few short hours together, she'd been bombarded by her attraction to him and wrestled to keep herself at a physical distance. At the same time, her disappointment in his workaholic lifestyle was just as present. He was just as dedicated to the job now as he had been back then. But she couldn't ignore her fierce protectiveness where he was concerned. Missy was lucky she'd never made it to the house last night. If all this had come to light with her here, Ian would have had to separate the women before someone had gotten hurt. And by "someone," Bree meant Missy.

She entertained herself with fantasies of winning rowdy catfights. Eventually, she noticed the yelling had stopped. Bree didn't know if he had hung up the phone or if his anger had finally run its course. Either way, she wasn't going upstairs anytime soon. She flipped the television to a documentary on Pompeii and let her mind get lost in history instead of the eruption taking place upstairs.

About twenty minutes later, the dull thud of footsteps coming down the stairs roused her from the show. She turned down the volume and looked up in time to see Ian in the doorway. His face was stony and emotionless as he came over and dropped down onto the couch beside her.

Bree sat quietly and waited. He would talk when he was ready. She knew better than anyone that he didn't like talking about his emotions. It might take him a while to be able to voice his feelings about what had just happened. Even Bree wasn't sure she could find the words if faced with a betrayal of this magnitude.

"It's true," he said at last. His voice was steady and even. The yelling was done and now he was back to the even-keeled Ian she knew. "Missy is not having my baby."

At least now he knew for certain. "I'm sorry, Ian. Is there anything I can do?"

"No," he said dismissively. "Missy has done enough."

"I'm surprised she admitted to it."

Ian chuckled bitterly. "She didn't want to, I'm sure, but it's the kind of lie where you'll get found out eventually. I'd done my part by rationalizing away all my doubts, but eventually she would have had to start showing. Eventually, she'd have had to give birth to this baby."

That was a hell of a lie to pull off. Had she really thought it through? "Did she tell you what she intended to do? If the story hadn't hit the press, she couldn't have kept the lie going on much longer."

"She said she was hoping that we would stop using protection and she would actually get pregnant. If that didn't work, she was going to pretend to miscarry after the wedding."

Bree shook her head. "With so many women suffering through the reality of losing a child, I can't imagine her faking something that terrible."

"That's because you don't know the real Missy Kline.

All anyone sees is the sexy blonde in music videos and on album covers. I'm sure people think she might be spoiled or a diva. But the truth is that she's ruthless, especially when it comes to her career. She learned it from her viper of a stage mom."

"Is that why she did it? For her career?" Bree's career meant everything to her, but she had a limit of how far she would go to be successful. Most people did.

"That's not what she said at first. When I confronted her, she cried and wailed that she thought she was losing me. She said she did what she had to do to keep us together because she loved me too much."

Ian looked down at his hands folded in his lap. "That was absolute crap. I know what it feels like to have a woman love me and it was nothing like that. She barely knew me. She certainly didn't love me. Missy has never been interested in anyone but herself. The truth was that her last album tanked and she was scrambling. I had no intention of renewing her contract and she'd burned too many bridges to jump to another label easily. That's when her whole demeanor changed. She was buttering me up, using sex to get her way. I knew that much. What I didn't know was that she'd realized it wasn't working. Before I could end it, she'd cooked up the fake pregnancy to keep it going.

"That just turned into a publicity gold mine for her. Celebrity weddings and babies are big news. She started this whole charade to save her career, and it worked better than she'd ever imagined. The publicity about the engagement and the pregnancy boosted her mediocre songs to the tops of the charts. She'd sold the exclusive rights to our engagement and ceremony photos to *Celebrity Magazine*. The wedding was even going to be televised. Did you know that?"

She didn't. Natalie might have mentioned it, but Bree had spent last Monday in a daze after finding out about Ian getting married. "Sounds romantic."

"Doesn't it? Every step she took was cold and calculated. She was going to revive her career so I would resign her. And if not me, she would see to it that she made enough headlines to get some other label to do it."

"The whole thing sure backfired on her, though. Who's going to sign her now?"

"I don't care," Ian admitted. "It sure as hell won't be my label. The wedding is off and the minute she's fulfilled the final obligations of her contract, I never want to see her pinched face again. If anyone else is dumb enough to offer her a record deal after all this, they deserve what they get."

They sat in silence for a few moments, absorbing everything that had happened in the past hour. Apparently being held hostage by a blizzard was just the beginning. Finally, Bree spoke. "Well, I'm sorry about all this. There's nothing I can really say or do to make it better, but I wish that I could."

Before she could stop herself, she reached out and clasped his hand in her own. She expected him to accept the brief gesture of comfort and pull away, but he didn't. He tightened his grip on her fingers, sending a surge of emotions through her. She probably wasn't the best person to help Ian through a moment like this, but she was the only one here. She wanted to hug him. Comfort him. But was that dangerous with their biggest barrier suddenly removed?

"Thanks, Bree," he said, running the pad of his thumb over her skin. "I guess I should be happy the snow kept Missy from getting here. Can you imagine the three of us trapped in the house when this happened?"

She shuddered, but she wasn't sure if it was his words or his touch. "I would've had to cut a bitch," she said with a sly smile to help lighten up the situation. "Seriously, I know how important being a good father is to you."

Ian nodded. "I keep telling myself that everything works out for the best. A part of me is relieved. A part of me is so giddy to break things off with Missy that I want to skip through the house. At the same time," he added, a sadness creeping into the green depths of his eyes, "even though I didn't want Missy to be the mother of my child, I wanted that child just the same. Even though he or she was never real, it felt real."

"Of course it did. And you should give yourself the time and space to grieve for the baby, imaginary or not. You can't just blink and have the whole situation suddenly not matter anymore."

"Thanks for understanding. You're right, and that's how I need to think about it. I'm glad I'm here instead of back in Nashville. I think some people there would just pat me on the back and say to get over it because none of it was real."

"It was to you. So take the time you need. Do what you have to do. I think you should take advantage of the peace and solitude here to deal with all this. That way when you return home, you're ready to face the fallout."

Ian looked at her with a furrowed brow. "Peace and solitude? I don't even know what that is, much less how to take advantage of it."

"I'll tell you what it is. And how to get it. You made fun of me last night, but unplugging is the best thing you can do right now. You start by turning off your computer and your phone. Forward your business calls to your assistant if you have to, but you don't want the press and well-meaning friends pestering you about all this. Give yourself pure radio silence."

"Turn it off," he repeated, although he didn't sound convinced.

"Yep," Bree said with an encouraging smile. "It's easy. I'll show you how."

Six

Silence wasn't all it was cracked up to be.

Bree had sold the idea to him like it was the greatest thing in the world. Not true. Without technology to distract him, Ian found he was uncomfortable with his own thoughts. Bree had given him his space and he was drowning in it.

Less than an hour after unplugging from the world, he was suiting up for the cold and heading outside. He had too much nervous energy and too many thoughts swirling around in his head. When he was younger and had the same problem, his mother would give him a physical task.

Then, and now, there was nothing that some hard labor couldn't fix.

In the garage, he grabbed the snow shovel and a plastic tarp, then headed through the house to the front door. He opened it carefully, leaving a preserved wall of snow going about three feet up the doorway. He spread the tarp down on the wood floor to protect it from snow that might fall inside and melt.

This was as good a place to start as any. From inside, he thrust the shovel into the top few inches of snow and hurled them to the side of the porch. Then he grabbed a second scoop and flung it to the opposite side. Again and again he shoveled until he was able to step out onto the porch and close the door behind him. From there, he lost himself in the physicality and monotony of the work.

It took more than an hour to make a good path down the front steps to the road. It took another hour to clear in front of the garage doors and excavate Bree's SUV. They wouldn't be driving anywhere anytime soon, but if the snow started to melt then refroze in the night, it could turn to an icy shell around her car and damage the paint job. Maybe even crack her windshield.

The work had done wonders for his outlook. His arms and shoulders ached, but he had powered through the stages of grief in a rapid-fire assault on the snow in his driveway. The anger, the disbelief, the disappointment, the relief and the associated guilt came and went with every shovelful of snow. Two hours and three blisters later, Ian finally felt the mysterious sense of peace that Bree had mentioned earlier.

Resting his arms on his shovel, he admired Mother Nature's handiwork. He normally didn't come up here when there could be snow, so the sight of the familiar landscape transformed into a winter wonderland was stunning. The sun made the piles of snow sparkle like they were coated in a dusting of glitter. Icicles hung precariously from tree branches and the rooflines of houses in the distance. The chimneys of his neighbors puffed towers of gray smoke against the bright blue sky.

It was perfectly silent. No cars driving down the road in the valley below them. No people talking or walking around. Even the animals were deep inside their dens staying warm. He felt a sense of inner calm being out here that he'd never expected to find, especially after this morning.

When it was all said and done, he couldn't be angry anymore because he'd been given a second chance. A chance to marry a woman he really loved. To start a family with someone he cared about. It was a life he really hadn't given much thought to until Missy had reeled him into it. And now that he was free of her deception, the idea of a family—one the way he imagined—brought on an overwhelming feeling of hope.

That sense of hope was shattered as he felt something cold and soft slam into the back of his head.

Ian turned around to the sound of a feminine giggle and discovered Bree on the patio. She was armed with several snowballs and ready to go to battle. An innocent grin spread across Bree's face, but there was a wicked glint in her eyes. "It's a snow day," she argued.

"Aren't we a little old for a snow day? I don't recall hearing school was canceled."

She wasn't deterred. He recognized that determined lift of her chin. She had strong-armed him into turning off his gadgets and now she was going to bait him into having some fun.

"You need something fun to distract you from all this crap. It doesn't matter if we're eight or twenty-eight, we're going to play in the snow." She chucked another snowball at him and this one landed squarely on his chest.

"Oh, it is *so* on!" he shouted. He used his shovel to fling a huge lump of snow at Bree. It sent her scattering off the porch, giving him time to make a few snowballs to defend himself. He took a defensive position behind her SUV. She hunkered down behind a tall drift by the porch.

They lobbed attacks back and forth. Bree got him in the head once, but he fired back and nailed her in the rear end when she bent over to make more snowballs. She squealed in mock rage, kicking off another round of assaults. Ian was getting frustrated, though. They could go like this for hours. It was time for some hand-to-hand combat to make things more interesting.

With a commando-like roar that would've made John Rambo proud, Ian charged through the snow and tackled Bree into a drift. With a cry, they sank a good foot into the snow. Once she recovered, Bree playfully fought beneath him. They rolled around, burying themselves in a dusting of white powder and making the most distorted snow angels ever conceived.

At one point, she was able to push Ian off of her and he fell backward into more snow. She started frantically burying him as though they were on the beach, until he rose up, ruining all her hard work and tackling her into fresh powder beside them.

Laughing and exhausted, they finally stopped fighting. Ian couldn't help smiling as he looked down at Bree, pink-cheeked and grinning with the snow at her back. She looked so beautiful in that moment with her messy blond braid dusted in white powder. Not the perfectly airbrushed and digitally altered perfection of his former fiancée, but *real* beauty. Flawed and lovely.

He wanted to kiss her again. Last night had whet his appetite without giving him enough to feel satisfied.

And he realized at that moment, he could. Without guilt. He wasn't engaged. The mother of his "child" was nothing but a manipulative liar. Missy would probably keep the six-figure engagement ring he'd bought her, but it was a small price to pay for freedom. All the thoughts about Bree that he'd beaten himself up over in the past twenty-four hours were no longer off-limits.

Bree looked up at him, her bright blue eyes wide and inviting. Her lips were parted softly, her frozen breath escaping her lungs into the cold. He watched intently as her tongue snaked across them. She wanted him just as much as he wanted her. It could happen. He could have everything he'd fantasized about since she'd stepped out of her car yesterday. He just had to careful. He'd learned not to give anything more than his body to a woman. Because this was the woman who had taught him that lesson, he had to be doubly careful. He could make love to Bree while they were in the mountains as long as he remembered they would never work in the real world.

"I'm not engaged anymore," he said, stating the obvious.

"I know," she said, her voice breathy.

"Last night we had a million reasons why kissing was a bad idea. I hated to let you go, but I knew it was the right thing to do. Today, I can't think of a single reason why I can't kiss you again."

This was her chance. If she didn't want him—if she still believed he was just a thoughtless, self-destructive workaholic—she just needed to say no and he would respect that. But damn, he didn't want her to say no. He wanted her to say that she wanted him *despite* the fact that he was a thoughtless, self-destructive workaholic. That she couldn't focus on anything but how much she desired him. In the here and now, none of that other stuff mattered.

"Neither can I," she said with a soft smile.

Barely a second after the words escaped her lips, his mouth was pressed against hers. Bree wrapped her arms around his neck, tugging him closer. He reacquainted himself with her, letting his tongue and his hands roam across the familiar yet different territory.

Bree made soft sounds, her fingertips gently pressing into him and urging him on. The noises she made were such a turn-on. They reminded him of heated nights on an uncomfortable twin dorm mattress. Of nights when school, his music, food…nothing was more important than making love to Bree. There was no day so stressful that losing himself in her couldn't fix it.

He longed for that comfort again. Ian hadn't had a day this bad in a long time. He wanted nothing more than to find relief from the worries in his mind by forgetting everything but how Bree liked to be touched.

His body stretched along the length of hers, every hard inch of his desire very obviously pressing into the soft curve of her belly. Her body undulated beneath him, the tight fabric of her jeans creating a delicious friction. An aching throb of need was growing more and more intense. If they didn't go inside right now, he was going to make love to her in the snow.

He had no interest in getting frostbite on sensitive parts he might want to use again later.

Bree broke the kiss. "I'm getting cold," she said, nearly reading his mind.

"That's funny. I'm burning up." And he was. Every inch of his skin felt as if it was doused in kerosene and set ablaze by the heat of her touch. Of course, he wasn't the one lying against the snow.

Bree leaned up to kiss him again, a smile curling her lips. "Well, then take me inside so we can strip out of these wet clothes and you can warm me up."

Bree had lied when she'd said she couldn't think of a reason why Ian couldn't kiss her. Well, at least physically there were no barriers to him doing whatever he liked, kissing included. It was more like reasons why he *shouldn't* kiss her. There were plenty of those, starting with the most recent and obvious one—that he was emotionally rebounding—and ending with all the reasons they broke up in the first place.

Until this morning, she hadn't had to give the idea of her and Ian much consideration. There was an attraction there—their chemistry had always been off the charts—but nothing would come of it. He was engaged and starting a family, and she was a professional photographer who didn't intend on making a habit of sleeping with clients.

With his relationship with Missy imploding this morning, the major barrier to their physical impulses was gone. But that didn't solve everything.

Handsome or not, Ian was still a workaholic. He still had his business to preoccupy his time. Being trapped here in the mountains had put his impulses on hold, but it wouldn't last beyond the blizzard. None of this would. The minute they returned to Nashville, everything would fall apart. At best, she would get two, maybe three days with Ian. And she knew that.

But in that moment, when he looked at her with eyes blazing with desire, she didn't care. None of those reasons mattered anymore. She would deal with the ending of their relationship when they got to the end. But she wasn't going to let herself ruin the beginning worrying about it.

Not when she was standing in Ian's bedroom, each of them slowly slipping out of their cold, wet snow gear. His dark green eyes never left hers as he tossed his gloves on the bathroom floor and shrugged out of his coat. Bree did the same, only Ian reached out to take her clothes from her.

They'd left their boots on the porch, so it was easy to take off her socks and then peel the wet jeans from her body. It was at that point that Ian froze in place, watching her undress. Despite how much she wanted out of those cold clothes, she was going to take her time. She turned around, giving him a full view of her rear end as the denim peeled away and exposed the pink satin bikini-cut panties she wore beneath them.

Ian groaned aloud as she bent over and stepped out of the pants. She followed it with her long-sleeved shirt. When she turned back around wearing nothing but her bra and panties, Ian was standing exactly as she'd left him.

Walking over to him, she pulled his sweater up and over his head. He cooperated with a smile until she reached for the button of his jeans. Then his hand came to hers, covering her fingers and keeping her from going any further.

"You get into bed and under those covers," he said. "Your skin is like ice. I'll start a fire."

Bree pouted for a moment but had to admit that was an excellent idea. She sauntered over to the bed, slipping off the last of her underthings and crawling beneath the heavy down comforter. It was like slipping into a warm bath. She sighed as she snuggled down into the luxury linens.

Ian quickly went to work building a fire. In only a few minutes the fireplace just beyond the foot of the bed roared with flames. That done, he finished undressing and disappeared into the bathroom. Bree waited patiently, unbraiding her hair and combing her fingers through the blond waves left behind. He returned a moment later with a handful of foil packets.

Bree was surprised to see the physique he hid beneath those bulky sweaters he wore. Back in college, he'd been tall and lean but not particularly athletic in build because he spent most of his time playing guitar. Given that for the past ten years he'd mainly sat at a desk, she'd expected him to have a head start on middle-age spread.

Instead, she was rewarded with a hard, lean body with thick muscles twitching beneath his skin. He had more chest hair now; the dark sprinkle across his pecs narrowed to a trail down his belly. At that point, her cheeks flushed. His desire for her was no secret. Her palms tingled with the need to touch him, but he was just out of her reach.

He paused at the edge of the bed, holding up one of the condoms. "I'm trying to fight the urge to wear three of these at once. I'm feeling a little paranoid. Please don't take it personally."

"One is perfectly effective," Bree said, "as long as the woman in question isn't after anything but your body."

Ian's dark brows went up. "Bree, are you just using me for my body?"

"No," she said with a sweet shake of her head. "I fully intend to, of course, but at the moment you're out of reach."

Ian laughed and tossed the condoms onto the nightstand. "I feel so cheap." He eased back the blankets and slipped in beside her. His skin was blazing hot as he brushed against her. How was it possible that the man could produce so much body heat?

Bree groaned and pressed the length of her body against him like a nuzzling cat. Ian hissed for a moment when her ice-cold skin touched his, but he was gentlemanly enough not to pull away.

"You're freezing, Bree."

She ran her palm over the hard muscles of his chest and leaned in to give him a kiss. "Then warm me up."

"If you insist." Smiling, Ian rolled over, pressing her back against the mattress and covering her body with his.

The heat and the weight of him were soothing. When he dipped his head to kiss her, she forgot all about being cold. His touch heated the very blood in her veins, the spreading warmth awakening her long-ignored body's desires. She relished the slide of his tongue along hers. His every caress was expertly targeted to her most sensitive parts as though the almost decade apart had been just a blink of an eye.

When his thumb brushed over the hard peak of her nipple, Bree gasped. When he sucked it into the warm heat of his mouth, her back arched up off the bed. He was relentless in his assault, teasing her with his teeth and tongue as his hands glided down her hip and dipped between her thighs.

"Ian!" she cried as he made contact with her feminine center. He smothered any other sounds when he kissed her again. His tongue mimicked the movements of his hand, slowly sliding in and out of her mouth. She squirmed beneath him, panting as he drew her ever closer to the edge of her release, again and again, always backing away before she shattered.

Then he reached for the nightstand. Ian sat up to roll the latex sheath over himself, then slipped back between her thighs. He tugged the blankets up over his bare shoulders to keep them in the warm cocoon and then lowered onto his elbows. His mouth found hers again and with a subtle shift of his weight, he was pressing against her entrance. Teasing her. Toying with her despite the need he was responsible for building inside her.

But she'd already waited too long for this moment. Now, she would have it. Bree cradled Ian's hips between her thighs. Impatiently, she drew up her knees, gripping his hips and drawing him forward. He moved with her and before she knew it, she got what she wanted. Every inch of Ian was buried deep inside of her. The moment was familiar, pleasurable, memorable…perfect. It shouldn't have been. This wasn't a reunion. They weren't getting back together. They were just venting pent-up desires and emotions and frustrations on each other while the snow kept the rest of the world from existing.

But what would happen when the snow melted?

Bree closed her eyes and bit her bottom lip. It didn't matter. None of it mattered. In this moment she didn't want to let all those worries creep in. She just wanted to enjoy being in Ian's arms again. Watching him play his guitar and sing last night had built a need in her that only he could soothe.

Ian eased forward and thrust into her a second time with a sharp hiss. Bree rolled her hips, taking in all that she could. Her body strained and flexed around him, her muscles clamping down until he groaned.

"Nice trick," he said. "But we're not finishing that quickly."

Leaning down, he kissed her and started moving

at a quicker pace. Eventually, Bree had to tear her lips from his so she could cry out with each pleasurable drive into her.

They fell into an easy rhythm, her hips rising off the bed to meet his every advance. The pleasure easily built up inside her again, this time with more intensity than before. He had toyed with her so much earlier that this release might be one for the record books. She clawed futilely with her short manicured nails at the taut skin stretching across his shoulders. She was trying to find something to hold on to, something to keep her anchored when her orgasm hit like a tsunami.

It was coming. Her whole body tensed, and her mouth fell open into a soft "O."

"Yes," Ian coaxed, recognizing the telltale signs of her impending release. "That's what I want to see. Don't hold back, Bree. Come apart for me, baby."

He increased his pace and she hardly had a choice in the matter. In an instant, the dam broke and the waves of pleasure crashed in on her. She gasped, she cried, she thrashed and writhed beneath him. And when it all subsided, her eyes fluttered open to find he'd watched every moment of it.

"You're so beautiful," he said, looking down at her.

She didn't feel beautiful. At that moment she felt flushed and sweaty. Her hair was damp and plastered to her skin. Her lips were swollen from kisses and her core was throbbing from good use for the first time in a long time. She wrinkled her nose, smirking dismissively.

"No," he argued, dipping down to kiss her. "It's not up for debate. You're beautiful. Perhaps the most beautiful woman I've ever seen up close."

At that, Bree laughed and pushed her hair out of her face. "You work in the record industry, Ian. There's got to be a steady stream of *Tiger Beat* princesses and sultry songstresses in your social circles."

"I know. And?"

Bree's eyes widened and she swallowed hard. How could it be possible that she ranked up there with all the music stars at the Grammys? It was sweet but impossible. She reached up to his face and ran a fingertip down the bridge of his nose. "I think we need to get you some glasses, Ian."

With a growl, he flipped, rolling onto his back with Bree sitting astride him. Bree squealed with the sudden reversal, their bodies never disconnecting. "I don't need glasses and I'm going to prove it."

His hands gripped her hips and he started thrusting into her from underneath. Bree braced her hands on the padded leather headboard and moved with him. His eyes never left her face and in mere seconds, his jaw was tight and his fingertips were pressing insistently into the flesh of her hips.

If he wanted to watch her, she'd give him something to watch. Bree arched her back, running her fingers through her hair and thrusting her breasts out.

"Just watching you move like that..." He half spoke, half groaned, his words interrupted by the powerful rush of his release. She rode out the storm, finally collapsing onto the mattress beside him in a state of physical, mental and emotional exhaustion.

Ian scooped her into his arms and pulled her back against the hard wall of his chest. "Beautiful," he whispered, planting a kiss on her bare shoulder as they both drifted off to sleep.

Seven

"Aha!"

Ian poked his head out of the closet, the Monopoly game clutched under his arm. "Aha?"

Bree was in the kitchen, her back to him. She turned toward him and held up a handful of full-size candy bars. "You've been holding out on me, Ian Lawson. I found your secret stash!"

He laughed, shut the closet door and carried the game into the living room. "It's not a *secret* stash. It's an emergency stockpile. Are you telling me you don't have a kitchen drawer filled with candy at your house?"

Bree planted a hand on her hip. "Uh, no. I use my drawers for utensils and towels. Normal stuff."

"That's because you don't have Patty grocery shopping for you. She makes it her personal mission to keep me happy by buying me treats even when I don't ask. She may have gone overboard this time considering

I'd requested a bunch of healthy food this weekend for Missy. She probably thought I'd starve up here."

"Well, we might with what I've found in the fridge." Bree turned back to the drawer and opened another. "Oh. Here's a bag of mini candy bars in this one."

"Bring them. We can use candy bars instead of money for the game. It will make things more interesting."

"What?" Bree's nose was wrinkled in confusion, an expression that he'd always found undeniably cute and, at the same time, sexy.

Back in school, he would kiss the tip of her nose when she made that face. Now, he turned away and started unpacking the pieces of the game instead. They were far from that level of intimacy, despite having slept together.

"Each piece of candy can have a dollar value. Plain chocolate is worth five dollars. If it has peanuts, it's a twenty-dollar bill. Crispy pieces are a fifty. Dark chocolate is a hundred. And the five-hundred is…one of the full-size bars. How's that?"

"Gambling with chocolate. I like it. I get to be the banker." Bree came into the room with her arms full of candy. "You'll steal from the bank."

Ian frowned. "What if I get hungry?"

"It will cost you some of your winnings."

He loudly groaned in complaint but happily continued setting out the cards. "I'll manage the properties, then." He started laying them out on the coffee table by color. "Do we want to play the quick version?"

Bree looked up at him with an arched brow. "Why? What else do we have to do?"

A sly smile curled Ian's lips. He could think of quite

a few things they could do, none of which involved dice and paper money, but Bree had wanted to play a game.

She noted his devious expression and shook her head. "I hate to break it to you, but we are *not* going to lie around and do nothing but have sex until the snow melts."

Ian knew that much. Despite how easily Bree had fallen into his arms today, she'd practically launched right out of them when it was over. He'd fallen asleep spooning her, the drama of the morning feeling as though it were a million miles away. Then he awoke a short time later to an empty space beside him in bed. By the time he stumbled back out into the living room, Bree was showered, dressed and suggesting they play a game. Like their encounter had never even happened.

He decided to go along with it. For now. He wasn't entirely sure where they should go from here. He'd simply acted on instinct, claiming what he'd desired. There hadn't been much thought or discussion put into the decision. All he knew was that he was aching to touch her again. He didn't know if voicing that need would send Bree running into his arms or out into the snow.

"It's either marathon sex or I'll get back on my laptop," he threatened. It was a hollow threat, however. Ian didn't really want to get onto his computer. He would never admit to anyone, especially Bree, that he was enjoying his time away from technology. His calls were forwarded to his assistant. His out-of-office message directed people to contact Keith in his absence. General business operations at the studio were under control. That only left his personal accounts. Considering everything going on, he had zero interest in wading into those waters.

Before he'd shut everything off, he'd texted his mother

and told her he would be out of touch for a few days and not to worry. No one else mattered.

That left nothing but a rowdy board game to distract him from his thoughts about Bree. And that worked for a while. An hour passed quickly as they collected real estate. It was something easy and fun to do. Ian couldn't even remember the last time he did something as simple as play a game. It was nicer than he expected it to be, almost like stopping and taking a deep breath after running a marathon. And he had been running a marathon since he was nineteen.

Bree rolled the dice, then moved her piece to one of his green properties with a hotel. She groaned. "What's the damage?"

Ian picked up his card. "That will be fourteen hundred dollars. Or, if you prefer, your Snickers, your Butterfinger and four of the mini special dark bars."

"You've nearly bankrupted me." Bree handed over the candy with a frown. "All I've got left is this crispy rice bar. And you know what?" She looked up at him and popped it into her mouth. "I'm hungry. Game over. You win."

"Good. I'm hungry, too." Ian unwrapped a piece of candy and ate it. The day had passed in a blur of drama, snow shoveling, lovemaking and board games, but now it was time for dinner. "Let's see what we can come up with tonight."

He climbed to his feet with his winnings and dumped them back into the kitchen drawer to eat later. He opened the pantry door and looked inside. He didn't typically keep much there, but nonperishables would carry over from trip to trip, and as he'd mentioned, Patty sometimes went off script.

"Check the freezer," he said.

Bree opened the door. "Hmm. Popsicles, a bag of frozen biscuit dough and…" She stopped to reach inside and pull out something. "Two rib eye steaks. They look pretty new. There's no freezer burn."

Ian took the package from her. It was definitely only a few days frozen with a packaged date stamp of the previous Tuesday. "God bless Patty." A wire basket on the counter held a mix of potatoes and onions, and she'd bought some fresh vegetables. Together, they could manage an excellent meal. "Tonight, we eat like kings."

Neither of them were experts in the kitchen, but things worked out pretty well. They thawed the steaks in the microwave while the potatoes baked in the oven. While they grilled the steaks, they steamed delicate haricot vert. An hour later, they had dinner on the table, complete with a bottle of merlot from his stash.

The logs in the fireplace were crackling beside them as a fire warmed the dining room. The food was good and so was the company. Ian had hoped for a romantic weekend, but this wasn't what he'd had in mind. It was even better.

"I feel so guilty," Bree said after a few moments eating quietly.

"Why?"

"It's Friday night and I'm in the mountains eating a nice steak and drinking wine that didn't come out of a box."

At that, Ian had to laugh. "What's so wrong with that?"

"I haven't had a Friday night off in six years. Friday night is rehearsal dinner night. As we speak, the soon-to-be Mr. and Mrs. Conner are just wrapping up their rehearsal at our facility. In a few minutes, they'll be loading into a limo and heading downtown to have their rehearsal dinner at a fondue restaurant. I should be there for all of it."

"Who's taking pictures instead? Is the caterer pinch hitting?"

Bree laughed. "No. Amelia is doing prep work for tomorrow and finishing up the wedding cake. Natalie and Gretchen are decorating and coordinating with contractors like the florist and the DJ. We have a contract photographer we call for larger weddings or emergencies, like today. Willie is covering the rehearsal dinner and, thankfully, the ceremony tomorrow."

"So when was the last time you had a whole weekend off?" he asked.

"Uh…" She hesitated, looking up at the ceiling as she tried to calculate it. "Not since college, I'd guess. I might've gotten a weekend over Christmas when people don't want to get married, but that's about it. The first few years after we opened, we worked nearly every day. Now, I get Tuesdays and Wednesdays off. That's my weekend."

Ian understood how it went. Starting from nothing took years of hard work, jumping in the ring to do anything and everything that needed to be done. "Considering all the grief you've given me about working too hard over the years, it sounds like the pot is calling the kettle black."

Bree avoided immediately responding to his observation by taking a large sip of her wine. "Perhaps," she said at last, "but I love what I do. When you love what you do, you don't work a single day, right?"

He nodded. That was the difference, he supposed. Ian was working himself into an early grave because he had nothing else to do. He didn't have a passion for record producing urging him on. "What about your personal life? Do you leave yourself time for relationships?"

"If you're asking if I'm seeing anyone, no, I'm not." She gave him a crooked smile. "A question that might've been better asked this afternoon before…" Her voice trailed off, her cheeks flushing red. "But no," she said, clearing her throat. "I haven't had a serious relationship in several years."

Ian was relieved to hear that. He wanted Bree, but he didn't want either of them to feel guilty about what they did. Especially because he wanted to do it again. "Me, neither. I mean, the Missy thing aside. Before everything happened with her, I hadn't dated anyone for more than a few months at a time. And I wouldn't have bothered dating her if she hadn't dangled herself right in front of me where it was easy to grab."

"Well, you know what they say about low-hanging fruit. It isn't nearly as good or sweet as the fruit up high. You just have to be willing to work to reach it."

Ian chuckled. "Yeah, I've certainly been going for the low-hanging fruit. I haven't had time to work any harder at a relationship. It's a shame, though. If I got one thing out of this whole mess with Missy, it was that the idea of starting a family really appealed to me. I just didn't want to start it with her."

"I don't blame you."

Ian sighed and sat back from his plate. Despite their discussion, he'd managed to demolish everything they'd cooked and still had a hankering for something sweet. He might have to go claim some of his Monopoly winnings before too long.

He looked up and watched Bree as she chewed her food and looked out the window. She was as beautiful as always, but their conversation seemed to have brought her energy down a little. He couldn't tell if she was overworked, or if the lack of love life was bothering her.

"It sounds like we could both use a vacation," he noted, trying to perk up the discussion.

The sadness slipped away from her expression, her thoughts returning to the present. Bree smiled and looked around at the cabin. "What would you call all this?"

This might be the closest thing he'd had to a vacation in a very long time, but that didn't mean it qualified. It just proved to him that it took a blizzard to get him to relax. "I call it captivity. When I say the word *vacation*, I mean beaches, warm breezes and suntan lotion." He looked at her with a raised eyebrow. "Bikinis. Frothy drinks. Skinny dipping in a private splash pool at midnight."

Bree's eyes grew wider as he spoke until they were like giant blue marbles watching him. Her cheeks were tinged pink, her lips moist and open slightly. He could tell her mind had followed him to a tropical location with the two of them mostly nude. Then, in an instant, she stiffened up and regained her composure. "That sounds like a nice idea. You should go when you find a new lady friend."

"What if I've already found a new lady friend?" he asked boldly.

Bree took a deep breath, her shoulders shrugging slightly. "I think we need to survive this trip before we start worrying about another one."

"May I take your picture?"

Ian looked up at Bree with a frown. They'd loaded the dishwasher and cleaned up together, then he'd carried his glass of wine into the living room to relax.

Bree had picked her camera up off the coffee table and started tinkering with it. Their dinnertime conversation had sent her brain spinning. A vacation? Together? Yes, they'd had sex, but she knew this wasn't going to go anywhere. Did he? It didn't sound like it.

When life got problematic, Bree preferred the buffer of her camera between her and the world. Because there was only so far she could go from the temptation and complication of Ian, the camera was her best bet.

Judging by the look on his face, he wasn't expecting Bree to spring this on him. Especially after she'd awkwardly rebuffed his offer of a holiday in the Caribbean. "Why would you want to take my picture?"

She shrugged. She couldn't exactly tell him her initial motivation. At the same time, as big a mess as this weekend was, she wanted the photos to commemorate it. "It's what I do." Bree reached for her nearby camera bag and pulled out a different lens filter. She held the camera up to look at him through the lens, snapping a quick photo to test the light in the room.

Looking at the shot, she was reminded how photogenic Ian was. He was a handsome man in person, with penetrating green eyes and a square jaw covered in evening stubble. His features were masculine but refined. His dark hair was thick and wavy, yet kept short enough to stay under control. Photographing him, however, brought out an aura of confidence and power. There was an edgy male energy in his photo. And if she looked closely...signs of long-term exhaustion and stress. She recognized that look from her father. It was the kind of bone-weariness that came from weeks and months of working at an insane pace. Success at all costs.

And that was why she couldn't go to the beach with

him. Once they got out of here, things would be just like they were before and she'd be pushed aside for his work again. If she was going to make time in her own schedule for a relationship, she wanted it to be with someone who was willing to do the same.

"Do you want me just sitting here like I am? Or would you prefer me nude?" he added with a wicked grin.

Bree sighed. Of course he would turn her request into a sexual innuendo. He might be nearly thirty now, but she was coming to learn that most men's sense of humor stopped developing around fourteen. At least it got her mind off her worries for a while. "Clothes on, please. I haven't taken nude portraits since my college project on the human form. It's not really my thing."

"I mean, I don't mind," he continued, ignoring her protests. "I couldn't help but notice you admiring my stunning male form earlier today. If you want to blow up a photo of me and hang it over your fireplace or something, I totally get it."

"No nudes. And no huge egos, either. I need to be able to get your whole, inflated head in the frame." At that, she hesitated. What she would really like was a shot of him with his guitar. In her old scrapbooks, Bree had pages of photographs with Ian playing. At the coffee shops. On a park bench. In his dorm room. Even on stage during one of his only school performances before he'd quit. She'd really loved photographing him while he worked, and adding another picture to the collection seemed appropriate. "I would really like to take your picture while you play, actually."

At her suggestion, Ian frowned, just as she'd expected him to. "Last night was a one-night limited engagement. I don't intend to do it again."

Bree dropped the camera to her lap, a pout threatening to force out her bottom lip. She tried to hold it in. "Please, Ian. You can play whatever you want. Just let me take a few pictures."

He sighed, then leaned forward to rest his elbows on his knees and look at her. "Bree, I know that you still think of me as the Ian you knew in school. I do the same thing. I see you and think about spotting you in the crowd at the coffee shop or when you helped me study for my algebra finals. But we're not those people anymore. It's been a long time and we've both grown up. That person you remember—the charming musician with the guitar—is long gone."

"But last night…"

"Last night," he interrupted, "was just for old time's sake. Nothing has changed. I'm not suddenly going to grab that guitar and pick up my music career where I left off nine years ago. Those were just the dreams of a teenaged kid who didn't know any better."

And those were the words of a grown man made bitter by having those same dreams crushed. It made her sad to think that one person had the power to make him throw everything away. He'd disengaged himself so much from his music that he wouldn't even pick up a guitar. Certainly he could at least play for fun without thinking he was going to be a rock star one day. Bree enjoyed her photography and had moderate success, but she never expected to shoot for *Vanity Fair*. She did it because she liked to do it. Wasn't that enough?

"Will you answer me one question, then, Ian?"

She could tell he didn't want to, but he would for fear she might not let the subject drop. "One question. And then we let the subject go and you will photograph me nude."

Bree twisted her lips, holding back her irritation. "Why does having a successful record label keep you from playing guitar? Why can't you have both?"

His dark green gaze narrowed at her. "That was two questions," he noted, dodging them both.

"Damn it, Ian. Come on. I know you still love to play."

"Of course I still love to play. Picking up that guitar last night was like being reunited with a long-lost brother. Like coming home. If you have music in your soul, you can't just lock the door and throw away the key. It's always going to be there. I try to channel it into my artists, but it never really goes away."

"Then why do you torture yourself? Why don't you play if you want to?"

"Because it still hurts, Bree!" He shouted the answer, almost as though he might not get the words out if he didn't. His face contorted with surprise and irritation before he shook his head and wiped his palm over his face. "I'm sorry, I didn't mean to yell. I just... It's easier for me not to play at all. If I don't play, I can try to forget about all the plans I had that never came to fruition. I can tell myself it was just a phase I grew out of. That I wasn't that good so I didn't lose out on my big chance. That no amount of practicing—" his voice trailed off "—would've kept me from losing the most important person in my life."

Bree opened her mouth to argue with him, but then she stopped. Her eyes met his and there was no doubt in her mind that he was talking about her. She swallowed hard, trying to choose her words wisely. "You didn't lose me because I thought you weren't a good musician, Ian. I thought you were a great musician."

"Then I lost you because I gave up." He shrugged. "No one likes a quitter."

Bree placed her camera on the coffee table and settled next to him on the couch. She took both his hands and covered them in her own. "No. Not even close. I loved *you*, Ian. You happened to play guitar. But that wasn't all that you were any more than me taking photographs was all that I was or am. I loved your spirit. Your thoughtfulness. I loved that you always held the door for me and would help me haul my camera equipment no matter how far off into the middle of nowhere I wanted to go. I loved your smile. I loved the way you loved animals and how excited you would get about the idea of getting a dog once you graduated. I remember you had the breed already picked out and the name to go with it."

"Gibson," he said, the surprised expression on his face making it clear that he'd forgotten until that moment.

"There were a million things I loved about you that had nothing to do with your music."

His green eyes were nearly boring into her by the time she finished. It made her chest feel tight, like he was squeezing her rib cage in his fists. "Then why did you leave me?"

Bree swallowed hard. "I didn't leave you, Ian. You left me. You didn't do it on purpose, but losing your music changed you. Day by day, the Ian I knew disappeared and there was nothing I could say or do to get you back."

"I'm still here, Bree. I always have been."

"Then prove it to me. Show me that inside the CEO of SpinTrax is the man I used to love. The one who would do anything to make me smile." Bree pulled away from him, walking over to the closet where the guitar was stored. She carried it back to him, holding it out.

Ian hesitated. His jaw was tight, the muscles in his neck and shoulders like stone. His gaze flicked over the guitar, but he didn't reach for it. She could tell he wanted to, but it was an internal struggle she couldn't understand.

"Then don't do it for me, Ian. We haven't been in love for a long time and you don't owe me anything. But you owe yourself a lot. Do it for yourself. Play your guitar. Write some new songs. You might find that keeping your music alive isn't nearly as painful as holding it inside."

That was what it took for him to reach out and take the guitar from her. He slipped the strap over his head and held it for a moment. "What do you want me to play?"

"Play whatever you want to, Ian. I just want to capture the moment." Bree took a few steps back and picked her camera back up from the table. As she turned it on and adjusted some of the settings, she heard the familiar notes of a Kansas song begin. This had been one of his staples.

As he began to sing, his heavenly baritone filled the large room.

Bree moved back, crouching down to take her first shot. Framing Ian perfectly, she stopped short of hitting the button. Instead, she just watched. His eyes were closed, his fingers moving deftly across the strings. He sang with such emotion, the melancholy lyrics touched her as strongly as if he'd written those words himself.

She only took a couple pictures. Four at the most. She couldn't bear for the sound of the camera interrupting his song. Ironic, considering her desire to photograph him playing had driven this entire, emotional discussion. About halfway through the song, she dropped the camera into her lap and just listened to him sing.

The final notes carried through the room, followed by a resounding silence. The house suddenly felt empty without his music filling it. Bree expected him to immediately set the guitar aside, having appeased her, but he continued to hold it. His fingers flexed around the neck, his palm caressing the smooth wood.

"Thank you," he said at last.

Eight

Bree awoke the next morning to a familiar sound. At first she thought she was dreaming it, then she heard it again and knew it was real. Lying facedown on the mattress, she rolled over and tentatively opened one eye to see Ian standing beside the bed with her camera. Taking her picture.

She immediately shot up, feeling an unnerving cold breeze on her skin. She looked down and realized she was naked. She quickly tugged the sheets up to cover her bare breasts and prayed Ian hadn't gotten a shot of that. They'd spent the night together and her clothes were currently scattered around the room. Ian, of course, was fully dressed, putting her at a distinct disadvantage. Last night it hadn't seemed that important, but she hadn't expected to be the subject of a photo shoot first thing in the morning.

"What are you doing?"

Ian twisted his lips in irritation and lowered the camera from his face. "I was taking pictures of a beautiful woman while she slept, but the moment has passed."

Bree leaned over the side of the bed, scooping up her shirt from the floor. She pulled it on. "Why would you want to take pictures of me?"

"Why would you want to take pictures of other people?" he countered.

Bree frowned, an expression that brought the opposite reaction to Ian's face. "You don't like having your picture taken," he said.

She wrinkled her nose. "No, I don't."

"A photographer who hates having her picture taken. How is that possible?" he wondered aloud.

Bree smoothed out the wild strands of her hair and tugged the blankets even higher under her arms. The fabric of the shirt was thin and did little to make her feel covered. "I prefer to be behind the camera, if you must know."

Ian raised the camera again and snapped another picture before she could turn away. "Now that you mention it, I seem to remember you were always the one taking pictures in college. I didn't think much of it at the time because that was your thing. But I remember going through old pictures after you transferred to UT and being frustrated because you weren't in any of them. I guess this is a lifelong aversion. I just didn't notice it before."

It was hard for Bree to imagine Ian poring through old pictures, looking for her after she was gone. She thought he'd already forgotten her, even before she'd left. "I've been avoiding photos of myself since my parents bought me a camera for my tenth birthday."

"That's a shame. You're more beautiful than most

of the women I see in magazines. You should spend more time in front of the camera for a change. For the benefit of society."

She shook her head, ignoring his attempts at flattery. Instead, her thoughts drifted to last night's discussion of nude portraits. "Before these pictures...*benefit society*...you didn't take any shots of me naked, did you?"

"You were naked in all of them, but you were sleeping on your stomach. There's nothing to see."

Bree's mouth tightened. "If I see so much as a nip slip when I go over those images, Ian..."

He held up his hands defensively. "You won't, I promise. There's nothing on this camera but images of a golden angel sleeping in my bed."

She'd believe it when she saw it. Her glance shifted over to the bright streams of sunlight coming in the window. "What time is it?"

"About eight-thirty. I woke up at six today like I usually do. Yesterday was a fluke. I showered, dressed, made coffee and watched a little of the weather forecast. I've got some good news for you."

Good news? "You've made me breakfast in bed?" she guessed.

"No," he said, twisting his lips in thought, "but that isn't a bad idea. I should've thought of that."

Bree flopped back against the pillows. It was too early for a guessing game. "Then what is it?"

"The weather station is reporting it should get to almost fifty degrees today. I heard the snowplows going by this morning. They're expecting most of the snow on the plowed roads to melt. With any luck, we should be able to head home tomorrow morning."

Bree smiled because she knew she should, but for some reason, the news didn't make her happy. Somehow, being trapped in the snow was the ideal environment for the two of them. They'd spent so much time talking, getting to know one another again. It felt like old times, except that it wasn't. And that fact would be crystal clear the moment they arrived back in Nashville.

"That's great," she said, feigning excitement. "I guess we should make the most of our last day here then."

"You're right," he said, setting her camera on the nightstand. "Stay put. I'll be right back."

Bree sat patiently waiting for Ian to return a few minutes later. He had a tray with some fruit, toast, jam and coffee. Ian carried it over to the bed, setting it down between them and kicking off his shoes before sliding under the covers.

"Breakfast in bed!" he announced.

Bree leaned in to kiss him and he captured her, pulling her closer. She wanted to melt into him, to make the most of these fleeting moments, but she knew she shouldn't. The closer she let herself get to Ian, the more she would be disappointed when it all fell apart. "Be careful," she said as she pulled away. "You don't want to spill the coffee."

Ian reluctantly sat back and they both started to eat. Bree slathered her toast with butter and strawberry jam before taking a bite. It was sourdough bread from the loaf they'd used to make grilled cheese the first night. It had a bite to it that mixed nicely with the creamy butter and sweet jam.

"Can I ask you something?"

Bree hesitated, her toast hanging midair. What could he ask that needed an introduction like that? She'd been awake less than ten minutes and had had two sips of coffee. "Sure. What?"

"Well, Thursday night I have this industry thing to go to. Cocktails, schmoozing, maybe a little dancing. It's the kind of shindig that makes me completely miserable, but I'm expected to be there. I'm also expected to bring a date."

Bree's breath caught in her throat. Was he asking her to go on a date once they were back in Nashville? That was a big deal. It was as if he was acknowledging that the two of them might be viable outside of this cabin. He'd hinted at it with their talk about fantasy vacations, but this was real. Concrete plans. Bree wasn't nearly as certain of their longevity as he was. Sure, he'd played the guitar a couple of times. He was trying, but he was still a far cry from being the carefree Ian she remembered. Right now, she was just a distraction from his laptop. Could there really be more? She both craved and feared finding out the answer.

"I RSVP'd last week to go to this thing with Missy," he continued, unaware of the tension that had leaked into her muscles. "Obviously, that's no longer an option. I could go by myself, but I really don't want to face all those people on my own. Since I've unplugged, I have no idea how the fake pregnancy scandal is all going down, but I'm sure everyone will be whispering behind my back or feeling sorry for me. I thought if I showed up with a blonde bombshell on my arm, it might shut them up. It might also be a lot of fun having you there. What do you think? Would you like to go with me?"

Bree hesitated. She wanted to go, yet she was afraid to say yes. If Ian was trying to have a life outside work, she needed to support that, or she had no room to criticize. She didn't have to work Thursday night. She could go. She wanted to go. She just didn't know if she *should* go. A glamorous night out, champagne with important people, bodies pressed close together while dancing across polished marble floors… Was her heart strong enough to withstand a romantic assault of that caliber?

"Okay," she said at last.

A wide smile broke out across Ian's face. "Really? Awesome. I think you'll enjoy yourself. I can introduce you to some musicians. Quite a few will be there. Do you like Jack Wheeler's music?"

Bree's eyes got big. Jack Wheeler had once been a member of one of the biggest bands in rock. He was an icon. A member of the Rock and Roll Hall of Fame. He was also a photographer who had put out several books in addition to gallery showings and magazine spreads. Yeah, she wanted to meet him. That would be amazing. "Sure," she said, trying not to sound too eager.

That just brought the worry back into her mind, this time of a more frivolous nature. She was going to a party with rock stars. What was she going to wear? She felt her chest tighten with panic. She didn't dress up very often. For weddings where she was shooting, she wore black pants and a black blouse so she could move almost invisibly through the party. She wanted to get great shots but not at the expense of the people at the wedding. She might have a cocktail dress. Maybe. Perhaps Amelia did. They were close to the same size, although Amelia was doubly blessed when it came to "the girls." She'd have to go shopping. She didn't want to embarrass Ian in front of his peers.

"What's wrong?" he asked. "You don't look very enthused. You don't have to go if you don't want to."

"No, no," she argued. "I want to go. I'm just not sure what I'm going to wear."

"Judging by the women I've seen at events like this, something chic and sparkly. And if I can inject my personal preference into the equation, something on the shorter, tighter side so I can spend all night imagining you taking it off when we get home."

That brought a smile to Bree's lips. "I suppose I can manage that. I'll go shopping when I get back to Nashville. Or I'll raid Amelia's closet. She will know just what to do. She's the fashionista. I'm just the photographer."

"Always behind the camera," he noted, referencing their earlier conversation.

"That's how I prefer it."

"And *I*," Ian began, "prefer *you* without that top on." He lifted the empty breakfast tray and moved it to the nightstand before snuggling up beside her. "Here's to making the most of our last day here," he said before pulling her into a deep, passionate kiss.

The moment his lips touched hers, all her worries vanished. There were no parties, no rock stars, no fancy dresses and no painful past. Just him and her together, cherishing their last day in the safe haven of the cabin. Tomorrow, they would return to the real world. And despite how carefully she had tried to hold back with Ian, she knew she couldn't last much longer. Soon she would give in and be his, no matter what the consequences. She'd tried to be strong, but his touch and his words made her weak.

Resistance was futile.

Ian stepped out onto the front porch the next morning and took one of his last lungfuls of fresh mountain air. The roads were clear and finally open. Their time here was at an end.

For some reason that bothered him. He didn't know why. He should be happy to get home and return to work and life as usual, but suddenly his everyday life didn't seem that appealing anymore. It felt empty, like he was just a robot going through the motions each day.

It was just like Bree to be able to sow seeds of doubt into his life in only a few short days. He'd gone nine years without playing a guitar or picking up a pen to write a song. As long as he kept those thoughts from his mind, he was okay. Now, his fingers were achy and restless to get back to playing. That wasn't what he needed to be spending his time and energy on. He was a four-hour drive from Nashville and the personal and professional cluster that awaited him in the wake of the fake pregnancy scandal.

He wasn't looking forward to dealing with any of that, most especially dealing with Missy. She might not be his fiancée any longer, but she was still one of his artists. Until the final terms of her contract were met, he'd have to work with her, but it would not be much longer. In maybe another month, he could cut ties with Missy and never have to think about her ever again.

Bree came out onto the porch behind him, her camera equipment slung over her arms to load into her SUV. There was the other woman that would plague his thoughts. If Ian was smart, he would cut ties and not think about Bree again, either, but that wasn't going to happen. When it came to his college love, he was the dumbest man in the world.

"I can help you with that," he said, stepping into the driveway and scooping a heavy bag off her shoulder.

"I've got it, but thank you," she said with a smile. "I'm used to hauling all this stuff around on my own, you know."

"Is there any more?"

"Just my backpack and the tripod. They're in the living room."

"I'll go get them." Ian went inside, climbing up the stairs two at a time. He found her bag and the tripod and picked them up. He gave a quick scan over the house and didn't see anything else that belonged to her. He went back outside and handed her the last items to put in her car.

"I guess that's it," she said, stepping back to slam the hatch closed. Bree swayed nervously in her Converse, her hands buried in her back pockets.

Her hair was braided again today, the same way it had been when they'd played in the snow. He felt the memory threaten to ignite a fire in him, but now was not the time. He'd had all day yesterday to get his fill of Bree. Now, he would have to wait until Thursday, at least. Even if he wanted to see her, it would take days to manage the mess he'd been ignoring when he unplugged.

"It's been a wild couple of days, hasn't it?"

Ian stepped forward, wrapping his arms around her waist and tugging her against him. "It's certainly not what I expected when I came up here. My life is completely different driving down the mountain than it was driving up it."

She looked at him with a smile that showcased her full pink lips and straight snow-white teeth. "Life doesn't always turn out the way you plan. Sometimes, it turns out even better than you can imagine."

"This is way, way better." Ian leaned in to capture her lips with his own. Bree melted into him, every soft curve pressing against his hard angles. He wanted to pin her body to the SUV, strip off every inch of her clothing and make love to her one last time. "Can you stay just one more hour?" he murmured against her lips.

She shook her head, reluctantly pulling away. "No, I've got to get on the road. Yesterday I told Natalie I'd get back in time to help them break down and clean up the rest of the Conner wedding."

"You gain an hour going back with the time change."

Bree smiled, kissing him softly, then disentangling from his arms. "I've already factored that in. Sorry."

Ian nodded. "I tried. Have fun cleaning up the reception hall."

"I'll see you on Thursday," she said with a bright, encouraging smile that seemed a little forced. She didn't seem to want to leave any more than he did.

"That's right," he said, nodding. "I'll pick you up about seven Thursday night."

"I'll be ready. Don't forget to take your guitar home with you," she added. "After that party Thursday night, I want you to play for me again. This time, naked."

Her words were meant to be a promise of a seductive night to come, but Ian felt every muscle in his body involuntarily stiffen at her words. He didn't respond, he just smiled tightly. "Drive safely."

Bree hugged him, then pulled away to climb into her car. He moved back to the porch, watching as she backed out and then headed down the winding road to the highway. The minute her taillights disappeared around the bend, the ache of anxiety started pooling in his stomach.

What, exactly, was he doing?

He was living in a fantasyland. Ignoring all the signs that his pleasant river cruise was about to go straight over a waterfall.

This should've been the end. He'd told himself he

could handle this. That it was just going to be physical and everything would be fine. But now it was anything but fine. He should've waved goodbye to Bree and put their relationship back on the shelf where it belonged. Instead, he'd asked her to go to that party with him. He wanted her to go. He thought she'd have a good time. He was excited about the idea of seeing Bree in a slinky dress and extending this relationship beyond their time here in the mountains.

But that wasn't the problem. The problem was that he was just delaying the inevitable.

They weren't going to work out. He knew that the minute he'd laid eyes on her again. Things might seem okay when they were here in Gatlinburg, but back in Nashville it would fall apart. Because Bree didn't want Ian Lawson, record producer. She wanted Ian Lawson, the musician. She wanted to roll the clocks back nine years and pretend that SpinTrax and everything else he'd done in his life didn't matter.

Bree had pushed too hard. Harder than just a well-meaning person would. She'd pushed him to play. Pushed him to sing. Pushed to photograph him while he did. She'd asked him to write new songs. A moment ago, she'd asked him to play for her again on Thursday night. It was abundantly clear that Bree didn't want *him* with his contracts, business meetings and A-list musical roster. She wanted the fantasy that didn't exist, and she would do whatever she could to change and mold Ian into what she wanted.

That wouldn't work. The ship had sailed and Ian could never return to being the idealistic musician he'd been back in school. He had been young, ignorant of the world and so excited by the potential of his future. Once all those things come crashing down around you, there's no going back. He had grown up. He wished Bree would do the same.

With a sigh, Ian went inside and started closing up the house. He turned down the thermostat, shut doors, pulled curtains and checked locks. He quickly cleaned out the refrigerator of anything perishable and gathered up the trash in the garage so Rick could take it down to the dump later. Finally, he ran through his bedroom and bath, looking for anything left behind and then carried his bag into the entryway. He paused, looking at the guitar leaning against the wall by the front door.

Now he had to make a choice. He'd come to a fork in the road. If Bree were still here, she would needle him until it was loaded into his car. With her gone, it was only up to him. It was a tougher decision than he'd expected.

Ian was fighting with himself over wanting that same fantasy she did. It was easy to ignore his dreams when they were buried in the closet along with his guitar. At the same time, Bree spoke about his potential and his music so passionately that it made him want to believe that he could have his musical dream and his company. She insisted there was no reason he couldn't have both.

With her miles ahead of him on the highway, the realm of possibilities was starting to crumble. It sounded like a good idea. A perfectly nice idea. Yet he knew it was impossible. His company took up so much of his time, he could barely date. Before Missy crashed into his life, he hadn't had a date in months.

How could he possibly manage working at SpinTrax, dating Bree and rebooting his musical career? It was impossible. At least one of the three things would suffer and he was pretty sure he couldn't let it be his record label. A hundred people depended on that succeeding.

What would that mean for his future with Bree? She wouldn't tolerate being anything but number one on his priority list. That shoved his future in music to the bottom rung. Could he stand to play knowing it wouldn't lead anywhere?

As if the universe were answering his question, his phone rang. It startled him, having been off for the past few days, but he'd turned it back on as they were getting ready to go. He looked down to see his talent manager's name and number on the screen.

"Hey, Keith."

"Looks who's back in the land of the living. Did you enjoy losing contact with the modern world?"

Ian chuckled. He didn't think he would, but it had been easy to pass the time with a naked, willing Bree beneath him. Who needed Candy Crush when you had that? "I needed a break and I got one. Now I'm ready to jump back into the fray."

"Good because the fray has been anxiously waiting for your return. I don't know if I'm a talent manager or your public relations officer. Several magazines have called looking for exclusives on your side of the Missy story. Ryan Seacrest and Howard Stern both want you to call in to their radio shows. If I were you, I'd go with Seacrest. Stern would ask a bunch of creepy questions about Missy's sex life. I'd feel like I had to listen to support you, and I really don't want to know."

Ian sighed into the phone. "Anything important happen? Anything aside from the mess with Missy?"

"All your other artists seem to be doing fine. The only calls I've gotten in the past few days have been from Missy's manager. Big surprise. He's trying to push for a new contract because her numbers have improved."

"Not for all the tea in China," Ian said. "If she's such a hot commodity, let her jump to a new label. There's got to be someone out there that will take her on her numbers alone. They're not stellar, but she's not going to play the fair circuit anytime soon, either."

He bent down, grabbing the handle of his bag and carrying it into the garage to throw in the back of his Escalade.

"I'll pass that along," Keith said. "In the appropriate legal speak," he added.

"Thanks. I'm hitting the road in about five minutes and I'll come straight to the office. I need to make a few quick pit stops, but I'll see you in a few hours."

"Can't wait for you to come back," Keith said. "See you soon."

Ian hung up and went back into the house. Talking to Keith made him feel normal again. His business was what drove his life and he was ready to get back to it.

In the living room, he glanced once more at the guitar. There was no room in his life for it, but he couldn't bear to leave it behind. Just like with Bree.

In the end, the guitar went in the back of the car with everything else.

Nine

"Wow." It was all Ian could say.

Bree arched an eyebrow at Ian. "Wow? Really?" She looked down at her outfit in confusion.

"Yeah, wow," he repeated. She looked incredible. How did she not know that? He'd expected her to choose something black, slinky but conservative. It was red. Fire-engine red. And lace. The dress had a conservative collar, long sleeves and a hemline just above the knee. Even then, it was the sexiest thing he'd ever seen. To start, it fit like a glove. It was also sheer. Except for the appropriately placed red fabric panels that ran down the front and back, the rest was see-through. He could see her pale skin peeking through everywhere else, including along each side. Panties...were an impossibility. And his mouth went bone-dry with the revelation.

"It's new," Bree said with a shy shrug. "The girls took me shopping and helped me pick it out. Will it be okay for the party? I know you said sparkly, but sparkles aren't really my thing."

Ian shook his head furiously. This was way better than sparkles. "This is fine. It's great. Amazing. You look incredible in it. Actually, we can even skip the party and stay home, you look so good."

Bree smiled, her bright red lipstick a shock of color against her pale, flawless skin. Her blond waves were pinned back into a chignon at her neck, a few loose strands along her face. She was wearing nude pumps and no jewelry. She didn't need anything else. She shined like a jewel all on her own.

"You're not that lucky," she said. "You promised me a party with rock stars and I intend to have it."

"If you insist. Are you ready to go?" If she was, they needed to go now, before he changed his mind and ravished her on the gray leather sofa he could see over her shoulder.

"I am." Bree reached to pick up a nude beaded clutch and stepped out onto her porch. She locked the door and he escorted her to the Escalade.

The party was being held in a Brentwood mansion ten miles outside of the city center. It was the home of former country music star and music producer Luke Chisholm. Luke had made his millions, burned out and dropped out of the music scene for several years. He'd reappeared four years ago, starting his own record label, like Ian. They would've been rivals if they didn't target different artists. Ian was after rock and pop music, a rarity in Nashville. Luke, like so many others, specialized in country and bluegrass music. Because of that, they had developed a friendship, always talking about collaborating with their artists but never getting around to it.

It didn't take long to get to the party and Ian was

glad. Just sitting beside him in the car, Bree was a distraction. The hem of her dress crept higher when she sat in the Escalade, tempting him with creamy thigh for one mile after the next. He almost missed his exit from sneaking peeks of her as he drove.

As they pulled up into the circular driveway of the mansion, they were greeted by a valet. Ian got out of the car, turned over his key, opened Bree's door and took her arm. They started up the stairs to the entrance.

"So, is this party for something in particular?" Bree asked as they approached the front door.

"Not really. Luke usually throws a party once or twice a year, no occasion. I always try to make it to his. It's for social mingling, mostly. A little business. There will be a mix of business guys like me, some artists, other industry people..."

"Interesting," she said, although she didn't look impressed. "Any drunk karaoke singing?"

Ian chuckled. "No. But with half the music stars of Nashville in attendance, it would be one hell of a performance, drunk or not."

A man in a tuxedo greeted them at the door and directed them through the marble foyer into the backyard.

"It's outdoors?" Bree asked with worry furrowing her delicate brow. "I didn't bring a coat. Or much of a dress, for that matter. Who holds an outdoor party in the winter? This isn't California."

Ian leaned in to Bree's ear. "I'm sure Luke has it under control. He takes care of every detail. Look," he said pointing at a few women just outside the glass. "Those ladies don't look cold."

A set of French doors opened up to a pool complex. A large semicircular pool sprawled out in front of them, crowds of people milling around it and standing on

Plexiglas platforms hovering over it. Scattered around the area were tall gas space heaters. As they stepped outside it almost felt warmer than it did inside the house.

"This is beautiful," Bree said, her gaze moving over the twinkling lights in the trees, the tables draped with rich fabrics and the floral arrangements that seemed to reach for the sky. "Don't be offended, but I'd much rather be here as a photographer than a guest. I really want to take some pictures of this setup. And the flowers. Gretchen would just love it. It makes me wonder what florist they're working with. But…I won't," she added with a shy smile. "I'll be cool. I don't want to embarrass you."

That made Ian chuckle. His Bree was many things, but cool wasn't how he'd describe her. She was much more comfortable behind the lens than strutting around in front of it, but he wanted to change that. A quick glance around was enough to prove that she was easily the most beautiful woman at the party. She should be as comfortable in front of the lens as behind it. "You didn't smuggle that big camera of yours in that tiny purse, did you?"

She smiled. "I wish I had, but I'm no Mary Poppins."

"Too bad. Without it, you'll just have to play my hot date tonight." He slipped an arm around her waist, pulling her close enough to kiss. Instead, he leaned in and whispered into her ear. "And if I find you in a corner talking to a photographer, I'll find a…creative…way to punish you later."

"Yes, sir," Bree said with a smile that indicated she wouldn't mind.

They stepped into the crowd, melting into the throng of well-dressed and powerful people. When he first got into the business, he'd been starstruck. Now it was just another day at work. On the far left, he spotted the nearest bar. "Would you like me to get you a drink?"

"Sure. Bring me a white wine. Chardonnay if they have it."

"You got it." Ian leaned in to press a quick kiss to her cheek and pulled away. There were several people in front of him in line, including Luke, the man throwing the party.

"If you're picking up the bar tab, shouldn't you be able to skip the line?"

Luke turned, a smile crossing his face when he saw Ian. They shook hands. "You'd think so. But I'm okay with waiting. It let me run into you, for one thing." The smile faded for a moment. "How are you, Ian?"

Ugh. That. Ian had tried to avoid the topic of the Missy debacle, but it was inevitable that it would pop up at an event like this. The music industry in Nashville was a small world. Everyone knew everyone's business. "I'm fine, really. The whole thing seems sort of surreal at this point."

"I knew Missy was a handful, but I never expected she could do something like that." Luke shook his head. "You know, she's been sniffing around my label this week. Her manager called the other day wanting to talk about Missy branching out into country music. I laughed at him."

Ian winced. "I'm sure you're not the only place she's called. I keep waiting to bump into her here. It's the perfect hunting grounds for an artist in need of a contract."

"Oh, she's here somewhere." Luke stepped up to get his drinks, then waited as the bartender poured two for Ian. "I saw you come in with a pretty lady. You'd better hope Missy didn't see you."

Ian shrugged. "I don't care what Missy thinks. After

the week I've had, I deserve to have a beautiful lady on my arm who isn't crazy."

"Right you are." Luke laughed. "But watch out for Missy. She will make it out of this scandal one way or another. Hopefully it won't be by climbing over you to get there."

"I will." Ian was glad he wasn't the only one who could see Missy for who she really was.

"Listen, call me next week and we can chat. I've got to get this drink back to Mrs. Chisholm."

Ian nodded, waving at Luke before picking up his drinks and turning in the direction he'd come. His eyes found Bree in the crowd, then he froze. A feeling of dread washed over him. Luke was right. Missy was not only here, but she had Bree cornered.

The two women were talking, but he could tell it wasn't idle chatter. Missy looked like she was on the verge of losing it. Taking her rage out on Ian's date wouldn't be out of character for her. They were far too close to the edge of the pool for any sort of squabbling. One or both would end up in the frigid, illuminated water.

As fast as his feet could move him through the crowd, he arrived at Bree's side. "Missy!" he said, interrupting whatever conversation they were having. Ian handed Bree her glass of wine and then wrapped his arm around her waist. He took two giant steps backward, putting some breathing room between them and Missy and moving that much farther away from the water's edge just in case. "I didn't expect to see you here tonight."

Missy crossed her arms over her chest, pushing her breasts up to the point of indecency. She was wearing red, too, although her dress was lacking the elegance of Bree's. It was satin, tight and short, with a plunging neckline. "You didn't think I was just going to tuck my tail in and run, did you?"

He wasn't that lucky. "Of course not. Why should you be ashamed of lying and manipulating everyone in your life, especially me? Now, if you'll excuse us…" Ian tried shifting them away from Missy.

"You can walk away from me, but this isn't over, Ian," Missy said ominously.

He sighed, turning back to face her. "Yes, it is. And there's nothing you can do about it, at least not here if you want a new record deal from anyone at the party. Goodbye, Missy."

Before she could say anything else, he propelled Bree in the opposite direction, following closely on her heels. They were on the other side of the party before they stopped.

"Thank you for rescuing me," Bree leaned in and whispered against his neck. "I thought she was going to throw me in the pool. This dress cost me way too much to get ruined the first time I wore it."

"Don't thank me. It's my fault she came after you." Ian took a deep breath. Less than ten minutes into the party and things were going downhill fast. "What did she say to you?"

"Eh." She shrugged. "The usual jealous woman stuff. Who am I? What am I doing coming to this party with you? Do I know who she is? Nothing very original. You interrupted before I could say something ugly to her."

Ian was glad he got there in time. Missy had a short fuse and no shame. He didn't want her ruining this night for Bree. He could already tell the party was going to be a lot of fun with her by his side. He usually spent most of his time conducting business and checking his phone. Tonight, he didn't have the urge to do either. He wanted to take Bree for a turn on the dance floor and introduce her to everyone. He wanted to feed her a chocolate-covered strawberry from the dessert table and snuggle with her by the fire pit.

"I'm sorry about Missy, Bree. I promised you a fun night, and after that scene, you're never going to want to come with me to another one of these things."

"Missy hasn't scared me off yet. And actually," Bree said with a smile, "all you promised me was a chance to meet Jack Wheeler."

He had said that, hadn't he? "You're right." He looked up, scanning the crowd, and found Jack sitting nearby with a group of other musicians she would probably be equally excited to meet. "Come with me," he said, taking her hand. "I'm going to do my part and introduce you to Jack."

"And then what?" she asked.

"And then I'm taking you home and slowly peeling you out of that dress."

Ian kept his word. They spent another hour or so at the party, chatting with enough stars to make Bree's head spin. And then they made a quick exit.

She expected Ian to take her back to her town house, but instead, he drove back into the city and the center of the music district. "Where are we going?"

"To my place."

They eventually pulled into the parking garage of a tall residential building. Ian pulled into his reserved space and escorted her to the elevator that took them up to his penthouse.

"Now it's my turn to say 'wow,'" she said as they stepped into the marble foyer. There was a stone compass star on the floor of the round entry and a sparkling chandelier overhead. "This is amazing."

Ian led her into the modern kitchen with black cabinets and gray, concrete countertops. "Thanks. I'll give your regards to my decorator. She fretted over it and almost no one ever sees it but Winnie and me. Hell, I barely see it."

Bree approached the kitchen, running her fingertips along the counter. "Is Winnie here?"

Ian shook his head. "She's not a live-in employee, although she has a room in case she needs to stay over. She'll be back in the morning, so no stumbling into the kitchen naked for a cup of coffee."

"Hmm…" Bree said thoughtfully. "You think you're going to keep me here all night, do you?"

"Yep," he said, reaching into the wine chiller to pull out a bottle. "I'm certain of it. Because I'm not driving you home until I leave for work in the morning." He poured two glasses of chardonnay and handed one to her.

"In that case, I'm losing the heels." Bree kicked out of the stilettos, sighing with bliss to be flat on the ground once again. The shoes were hot, no doubt, but she really just preferred her Converse. She even had red ones that would've matched the dress, but she didn't need Amelia freaking out over her major fashion faux pas.

"That's better for the tour, anyway." Ian started through the house, pointing out details as they walked. He had the entire top floor to himself, with an unnecessary number of bedrooms and bathrooms in addition to an office, a gym and a movie theater.

"Ian, why such a big penthouse? You could have someone secretly living here and you wouldn't ever know it."

Ian shrugged. "I didn't want a house. I wanted to be in the city, close to the studio. I liked the features. And I guess I figured that someday I might need the other rooms for a wife and family."

"Or Missy and all her assistants?"

Ian looked at her with a pinched, irritated expression that quickly faded to a smile. "Or *that*. Dodged a bullet there." At the end of a corridor, Ian opened a door and let her step in ahead of him. "This is the master suite," he said, slipping out of his suit coat and tossing it across the back of a chair.

It was another beautiful space. After being at his rustic cabin for several days, it was interesting to see how modern his apartment was. Glass, chrome, polished stone and leather. The stark-white king-size bed was on a raised black marble platform. It had a tall white suede headboard and another chandelier hanging over the bed. There was a sitting room with a television and a fireplace, and beyond that, she could make out the master bath. It was larger than her living room and she had what she thought was a pretty spacious town house.

Bree stepped onto the raised platform and sat on the edge of the bed to sip her wine. "Pretty impressive," she said. "A far cry from your dorm room and that lumpy twin bed."

"Thank goodness." Ian sat beside her as she sipped the last of her wine and placed the empty glass on the platform by her feet. Together, they looked out through the wall of windows to the skyline of downtown Nashville. The glowing twin spires of the Batman Building and the bright red L&C sign on the top of the Life and Causality Building made for quite a view.

She was lost in the twinkling lights of downtown when she felt Ian's hand at her neck. He found the snap and the zipper and ran it down the long curve of her back. She closed her eyes, relishing the feel as his fingertips followed the same trail, caressing her skin down to the hollow at the base of her spine. She shivered, his touch sending a wave of goose bumps across her arms and legs. Those same goose bumps immediately vanished when Ian pushed her sleeves off her shoulders and placed a searing kiss on her bare skin.

Ian kept pushing until the dress was peeled down to her waist, exposing her breasts. She slipped her arms out of the sleeves and arched her back to lean against his chest. His hands immediately moved over her breasts. She gasped as his fingertips teased the hard pebbles of her nipples.

"You look amazing tonight," he whispered, letting the tip of his tongue graze her earlobe. "I've never wanted a woman as much as I want you right now."

"Oh, yeah?" she purred, letting her hand slip in between his thighs to confirm it.

Ian groaned loudly, his hand moving quickly to her wrist to tug her away. "Not yet." He stood up, looking down on her as she sat on the edge of the bed. He placed his hands on her shoulders and pushed until she was lying back on the bed. His hands quickly went to her hips, gripping the bunched fabric there to tug it down her legs.

He stood back up, looking at her completely nude body with a blazing heat of desire in his eyes. Slowly, he pulled off his tie and unbuttoned his dress shirt.

Bree slid back on the bed until she reached the pillows. "Don't make me wait any longer," she said. She was immediately joined by a naked and sheathed Ian, his body covering every inch of hers. She didn't hesitate

to part her thighs and allow him to slip between them.
He surged forward until he was buried deep inside her.

She closed her eyes and savored the feeling. Not just
the distinctly feminine experience of sex, but the intimacy it built between them. It was something she had
lacked with other partners but never with Ian. And especially not now. She had never felt closer to a man in
her life than she felt to Ian at this moment.

They moved together like they were one. He tasted
her mouth, her breasts, her throat, drawing soft cries
from her lips. She clung to him, tensing her muscles
around him as she felt her release build up inside her.

"Ian!" she gasped.

"Let go," he whispered against the soft line of her
jaw. "Just let go."

Bree felt herself giving in. Not just to his request to
let go, but to the thoughts that were racing through her
own head. She'd resisted. She had good reason to. But
in the moment, she didn't want to hold back anymore.

Bree wanted her relationship with Ian to last beyond
tonight, beyond her gallery showing this weekend. She
wanted to give this a real try, and Ian's actions had encouraged her to think it was a possibility. He really
seemed to enjoy the time he spent with her away from
work. She'd spied the guitar in his bedroom when she
walked in, so perhaps he was getting some pleasure
from embracing his music again. He seemed happier.
His smile was enough to make her heart ache and her
chest tighten.

She could really lose her heart to Ian. Just a little life
balance for them both could make all the difference in
the success of their second chance.

And she wanted this to be their second chance. Not
just a fun fling. It meant too much to her for that. And

if she was honest with herself, she had already lost the fight. Bree loved Ian and she had since she was eighteen years old. Seeing him again had brought everything back to the surface and she was tired of fighting her feelings.

As Bree unraveled the protective wrappings around her heart, she felt her body start to unravel also. The swell of emotion and pleasure built up inside of her so quickly, she could barely react before it was upon her.

"Yes, Ian," she whispered, clinging to his shoulders as the spasms of her release rocked through her body. "Love me!" she cried again and again until it was over. A moment later, Ian found his own release, shouting her name into the delicate crystal fixture overhead.

He was too wrapped up to understand her pleas. Love me, she'd begged, but it had nothing to do with his physical touch and everything to do with his heart.

Love me.

Ian woke early the next morning, as usual. Any other morning, he would reach for his phone to check the time, read over his email and then hit the ground running. His routine rarely varied—shower, coffee then out the door by seven and in the office by seven-thirty.

But not today.

Today, when he opened his eyes, he wasn't propelled out of bed by the cold sheets beside him and the peek of sunlight through the windows. All he could see was golden-blond hair. Bree was curled against him, comfortable and warm. Her soft, rhythmic breathing was soothing, tempting him to fall back asleep with her in his arms. And he wanted to. He had zero interest in getting up and starting his day. He wanted to stay right where he was for as long as possible.

Propped up on his elbow, he watched her sleep for a few moments. She had the same serene expression he'd tried to catch with her camera in the mountains. The soft, pouted lips…the rose-tinted cheeks…the dark blond lashes against her peach skin… Ian wanted to memorialize the moment so he could have it with him always.

Of course, there was another way.

Ian's chest constricted when he thought about it. Having Bree here, waking up with him every morning, was exactly what he wanted. That was better than a picture any day. He wanted her right here when he woke up and in his arms when he fell asleep. Knowing she would be at his apartment each evening was a powerful driver for him to go home when the normal workday was at an end. He desperately needed balance in his life, but for years, he'd had no reason to go home.

She might drive him mad at times, but no one else challenged him like Bree did. No one understood him, cared for him and maybe even loved him the way Bree did. She had touched him in a way no other woman had before. They may have spent far longer apart than they'd spent together, but he wanted to change that.

He was overwhelmed with the sudden urge to shake her shoulder and wake her up. When her blue eyes opened and looked up at him, he knew exactly what he wanted to say. It might be crazy, but he wanted to tell her that he loved her and ask her to marry him. It wasn't very romantic. He didn't have a ring or flowers or, hell, pants on, but the words were on the tip of his tongue, begging to leap out of his mouth.

When he'd proposed to Missy, there had been an ache of worry in his gut. He hadn't wanted to do it. Every nerve in his brain was screaming for him not to do it. But now, there was only excitement. He was at peace with his decision. All he had to do was wake her up and say the words.

Bree made a soft cooing sound in his arms and rolled onto her back. A moment later, her eyes fluttered open and slowly came to focus on his face. Her nose wrinkled in sleepy confusion. "Hi," she said. "What's the matter?"

"Nothing is the matter." His heart started racing in his chest as the adrenalin surged through his veins. "I just wanted to ask you a question."

Bree rubbed her fists into her eyes and yawned. "What?"

"Bree, I…" he began, and then, in that moment, he lost his nerve. Ian hadn't changed his mind, but he knew Bree deserved better. Thirty years from now when she told this story to their grandchildren, he didn't want it to be embarrassing. He didn't want Bree to have to leave out the details about how they were naked in bed and she was half-asleep. He needed to do this right. The ring, the flowers, the perfect moment…

Her show.

That would be perfect. She'd worked so hard on it. What better way to wrap up her big night than to propose in the middle of the gallery?

"Ian?" Bree roused him from his plans with a delicate hand to his cheek. "You *what*?"

He smiled, picking up her hand and placing a soft kiss against the palm. "I want pancakes for breakfast."

She chuckled and shook her head. "Pancakes, huh? You made it sound like you were about to propose marriage or something. So serious looking. Well, how about you and I climb into that gigantic shower of yours and, afterward, I will make you pancakes."

"Sounds great," Ian agreed. And it did. If he could start every day like this for the rest of his life, things would be just about perfect.

Ten

He was late. This was not how he needed to start off tonight.

Ian shut down his laptop and slipped his phone into the holster at his hip. He was putting his suit coat on when he caught movement out of the corner of his eye.

Missy.

She was standing in the doorway looking like she'd walked right out of a music video. She had on leather pants, a red-and-black corset top and five-inch heels. Her makeup and platinum-blond hair were camera-ready. It was a little much for a Monday night, but Missy lived by a policy of go big or go home.

Even then, with her fake breasts nearly spilling over the top of her corset and her pouty moist lips, Ian had a hard time imagining he'd ever slept with Missy, much less nearly married her. After spending time with Bree, a more natural beauty, Missy looked overdone. Forced. She was trying too hard.

He wasn't sure why she'd gone to so much trouble. Judging by the strained, angry expression on her face, she wasn't here to win him back. Ian knew this moment was coming, eventually, but why did it have to come right now?

Ian silently cursed and rounded his desk. He did not have time for this. He was already late for Bree's gallery show. He couldn't miss it. Not only was it superimportant to her, but he knew it meant more than that. Bree was waiting, just waiting, for the other shoe to drop. For him to blow off something for work. She had been holding her breath since they had gotten back together. He couldn't screw this up.

"Ian," Missy said, strolling leisurely into his office. "Now that you're home, we need to talk."

Ian sat on the edge of his desk, his arms crossed over his chest. "There's nothing to talk about, Missy. I told you on the phone it was over."

Missy laughed, a low sultry sound that was a trademark of her albums. It was extremely unnerving to Ian.

"Ian, do you really think I'm here to win you back?"

He swallowed. "I really don't know why you're here, Missy."

"Well, you can stop worrying your little head about that. I'm not about to get on my knees and beg you to love me. Our relationship was nothing more than a fantasy I concocted to sell records. And it worked."

She was right. Even despite the scandal, her sales numbers had climbed to near historic highs for her at SpinTrax. Ian would never understand the public. He didn't know if her fans just didn't care about the way Missy lived her life or if the train wreck was part of the appeal. A part of him had hoped she'd just check into rehab and fall off the radar for a while, but no such luck. She was soaking up the publicity, both good and bad.

"What's your point, Missy?"

"My point is that I am still a valuable commodity. I'm not going to let you cast me aside, Ian."

He frowned at her. He should've known this was about business. It always was with her. "If you're so valuable, why don't you go to another label? Certainly there's someone else out there willing to put up with your antics for the money. Or—" he hesitated "—are you not worth the aggravation? Will no one else take you on, Missy?"

He could tell that he was right by the way her eyes narrowed angrily at him. She'd probably spent the past week with her manager trying to hunt down a new deal. If she'd been successful, she wouldn't be here right now.

Missy's face tightened, an unattractive red mottling her airbrushed face. Her bloodred fingernails were digging into her palms. He wouldn't be surprised if she scratched him with those claws. He slipped his phone out and set it beside him on the desk. If he needed to dial security quickly, he could.

"You're going to re-sign me, Ian."

At that, he had to laugh. It wasn't the smartest move, considering how close Missy was to the edge, but he couldn't help it. She couldn't make him do anything, and the last thing on Earth he was going to do was sign Missy to his label again.

"If you don't, I'm going to get a lawyer and sue you."

Ian's brow furrowed into a frown. "Sue me for what?"

"Sexual harassment."

Ian almost choked. It wasn't true. Not even remotely, but once a charge like that was thrown out there, it was hard to overcome in the court of popular opinion. "Please tell me, Missy, how I sexually harassed you. As I recall, you're the one who came to me, plying me with alcohol in your seduction plot. You're the one who pretended to be pregnant so we would get married. How is that me harassing you?"

"Well, you see," she said with a sly smile, "I didn't really want anything to do with you. I brought you that dinner as a peace offering. I never expected you to demand sex in exchange for another record contract. I didn't know what to do, so I gave into your insatiable sexual appetite."

"That's a lie."

Missy shrugged. "Only you and I were there. Prove which version of events is fact."

"How will you explain the fake pregnancy scandal?"

"You threatened me." Missy's dark eyes were wide and innocent, putting on a show for his benefit. "Even after I gave myself to you, it wasn't enough. You were still going to drop me from the label. You even said you'd ruin my career so I'd never work anywhere again. So I did what I had to do."

Ian shook his head. "Because marrying the guy who harasses you is always the best plan."

"People make dumb choices under duress. My lawyer will produce specialist after specialist who will get on the stand and tell everyone how I was being terrorized."

"Terrorized?" Ian could hardly believe this. Missy didn't have a stitch of evidence to back up her outrageous story, but with enough lawyers and enough money, it wouldn't matter. Either in court or out, she could destroy him. Destroy SpinTrax.

He took a deep breath to collect himself. He couldn't let himself get emotional. This was business and he was first and foremost a businessman. He wasn't going to let Missy manipulate him. She was threatening him because she expected him to lie down and take it. She figured she would get her way, just like she always did. But that would end here.

"Okay," he said calmly.

"What do you mean 'okay'? You're going to sign me to a new deal?"

He shook his head. "Absolutely not. There's no way in hell you're getting another contract from SpinTrax, Missy. Go ahead. Take me to court. Drag my name through the mud. I don't care. All you'll do is destroy the record label and put a lot of hardworking people out of a job. Either way, you'll end up without a record deal. You think you're a hard sell now? Just wait until the president of every record label sees what you did to me. Their lawyers won't let them touch you with a ten-foot pole. You might take me down, but you'll destroy us both in the process. Is that what you want?"

Missy's lips twisted as she tried to decide what to do. He'd called her bluff. He didn't want to lose his record company. He didn't want all of his employees to lose their jobs. But if it happened, it wouldn't be the end of the world. He'd make sure every one of his employees got placed at another label. They were all talented, dedicated people and it wouldn't be hard to find them another contract. The only person who would be out of work was Ian. And Missy. He was okay with that.

Two weeks ago, he wouldn't have felt the same way, but today, he just didn't care. Being with Bree had taught him that he wanted more from his life than just a successful business. He wanted a musical career of his own, even if he never achieved the level of success he dreamed of. Playing for others made him happy, be it for an audience of two or two thousand. He wanted a family and he wanted Bree to be a part of it. The engagement ring in his coat pocket was evidence of that.

That didn't mean he wanted to lose everything he'd built, but it wouldn't destroy him. He wouldn't let it. He'd done this once, so he could do it again. This time, he would have Bree at his side. The idea of it made him feel invincible. Let Missy just try to ruin him.

As calmly as he could, he looked down at his watch and realized how late he was for Bree's show. By the time he got there, it would nearly be over. He tried to maintain a bored countenance as he looked down. He didn't want Missy to mistake his anxiety over being late for concern about her threat.

"So, I'm glad we talked, Missy. It's been enlightening on several levels." He slid his phone back into the holster, stood and made his way toward the door to usher her out. "Have your lawyer call my lawyer and we'll move forward with this if that's what you want to do. Either way, this discussion is now over. I have somewhere to go and I'm already late."

"Meeting the wedding photographer?"

"Not that it's any of your business, but yes."

Missy flung her blond hair over her shoulder, lifting her defiant chin to look him in the eye. "I can't believe you brought her to that party the other night. You can point fingers all you want, but sleeping with the woman there to take our engagement portraits is pretty low."

"I'm not arguing with you about this, Missy. Our relationship is over. What I chose to do after that is none of your concern."

"From an international pop star to a lowly wedding photographer," she mocked. "Sounds pretty desperate to me."

Ian snorted. Even with half the male population lusting after her, Missy was incredibly insecure. And she should be. She couldn't hold a candle to Bree. "You'd know desperation when you saw it, wouldn't you, Missy?"

Missy's face scrunched up in anger. "You go to hell, Ian!" She spun on her expensive heels and marched out of his office.

"Good riddance," he said, stepping out into the hallway and closing the door behind him. He had to get across town to Bree's show and now.

Bree was a fool. She'd suspected it for a while now, but standing in the middle of the Whitman Gallery with a half-empty glass of champagne and Ian nowhere in sight, she was certain.

She hadn't noticed his absence at first. She'd figured he wouldn't be there on the dot anyway, and she'd been busy when the event had first started. The gallery owner had introduced her to the waiting crowd and she had spoken for a few moments about her collection and its inspiration. Then she'd made her way through the room, meeting people and chatting about her work. Before she knew it, nearly two hours had passed and there was no sign of him.

She pulled her flip phone out of the pocket of her dress, but it was just as she expected. No calls. No texts. No surprises. The show was almost over and he had stood her up again.

Bree slammed the phone shut and shoved it back in her pocket. She was trying not to let this ruin her night. She had worked long and hard to get to this point. A lot of important and influential people in the industry were here tonight to see her work. Big things could be on the horizon for her if she played her cards right. That meant she had to focus, smile and schmooze with the people strolling through the gallery. And she had. But as the night went on, it was getting harder to keep a smile on her face.

It helped that so many of her friends had come to support her. All her coworkers and even some of the couples who had appreciated the work she'd done for their weddings were in attendance. Both her parents had come, which was a miracle on its own. She'd figured her mother would show, but her dad's arrival had caught her off guard. He'd torn himself away from his construction business for Bree's big night. He knew how important it was to her. How could Ian not see that?

"Oh, Bree, this one is wonderful."

Bree pulled herself out of her funk to see Amelia beside her. Her eyes were focused on the large black-and-white photo in front of them. No wonder her thoughts had gotten so dark. She didn't realize she'd stopped in front of that particular portrait until that moment.

It was the photo she'd taken of Ian in the mountains. She hadn't planned on adding additional pieces to her collection this late, but once she saw the shot of him playing his guitar, she knew she had to include it. It might very well be one of her best pieces in the gallery tonight. She'd been proud of that shot. Now she was looking at having her most well-received piece being a photo of her ex. Of course.

"I've never seen this photo before," Amelia said. "I thought I'd seen all your work."

"It's a new one." Her tone was noncommittal, trying to keep Amelia from pushing the subject. In addition to this portrait, she'd also printed out the picture Ian had taken of her in bed that morning in Gatlinburg.

It was a beautiful shot with the morning sun giving a golden aura to her shape. Because she hadn't taken it, it couldn't be in her collection, but she was going to hang it in her apartment somewhere. He'd been right. There weren't enough photos of her.

"I really love it. Is that Ian playing the guitar? *The* Ian?"

Bree took a deep breath. "Yes, that's him. Soak it in. It might be all you ever see of him."

Amelia turned to look at her with a frown. "Why? What's going on? I thought he was supposed to be here tonight. I was looking forward to meeting him."

"I was looking forward to introducing you to him." Bree could feel unwanted tears start to form beneath her eyelids. She wasn't going to cry at her showing. She wouldn't. She could hold it together until she got home and could mope privately.

Amelia wrapped a comforting arm around her shoulder. The caterer and pastry chef of From This Moment was big on the power of love. She was a true believer, unlike Natalie, who thought the whole concept was bunk. Bree fell in the middle of the spectrum. She believed in love; she just didn't think that love alone could solve all her problems.

Bree hadn't mentioned how she felt about Ian to her, or anyone for that matter. If she had, Amelia would be telling Bree she had no doubt that Ian would charge in on his white steed and sweep her off her feet.

"He'll be here," Amelia reassured her. "I'm sure he got caught up in something, but he still has time."

He had fifteen minutes. Even if he showed up, it wouldn't matter. He would have missed the whole thing.

"I'll be fine, Amelia. Don't worry about me. Enjoy yourself. Drink more wine before the bar closes. I've got to go wrap up a few things with the gallery management before we're done."

Amelia departed reluctantly. The look on her face made it obvious that she knew Bree was just making excuses to be alone. The crowds were starting to dwindle and it was a cue for everyone to go home. Bree thanked the last folks as they made their way out, then sat down on the bench in the center of the room.

This part of the gallery was a white-walled rectangle with track lighting to illuminate the art. Bree was facing four pictures, each showcasing a part of Nashville that she loved. She had never been more proud of her work than she was tonight. Yet her heart was heavy. She'd wanted to believe that Ian meant what he'd said when he told her he'd be here come hell or high water. Just like she'd wanted to believe him back in school. But the results were just the same. She was alone. Forgotten. Discarded.

"Bree!"

She looked up to see Ian burst into the room. He looked panicked. Frantic. And he should. There were only five other guests in the gallery. Catering was breaking down. The party was over. And here he was. She supposed she should be pleased that he arrived at all, but at the moment, she just couldn't make herself appreciate that fact.

Bree stood slowly. She turned toward him as he approached her, but she didn't go to him the way he expected her to. She knew that by the way he stopped short of pulling her into his arms.

He stood awkwardly a few feet away, a bundle of white daisies in his hands. They were her favorite flower, but she didn't know if he remembered that or if it was just a good guess. Either way, a couple of flowers couldn't make up for what he'd missed.

"These are for you," he said, holding out the bouquet.

"Thanks." Bree accepted them, but it didn't do much to soften the hard, armored exterior she'd built up waiting for him to arrive.

"I'm so sorry I'm late. I can explain," he began, but Bree didn't want to hear it.

"You don't have to explain, Ian. I was expecting this," she said with a sad shake of her head. "I didn't want to be right. I hoped I was mistaken, but I knew how this night would end."

He looked mildly stunned by her cold response. Apparently he thought flowers and a good excuse would get him off the hook. "How does it end?"

"It ends with you going your way and me going mine. Just the way it should have when we left the mountains. You and I both know we were putting off the inevitable by trying to make things work between us."

"No," Ian argued, reaching out to touch her shoulder, but she pulled away. "Bree, listen to me. I was on my way here when Missy barged into my office and threatened to sue me. I dealt with her as quickly as I could and rushed over here. I didn't want to miss this. Tonight was supposed to be special. I wouldn't have deliberately ruined it."

Bree shrugged. It sounded like a pretty fantastic story, but the truth was it didn't matter why he'd missed the show. A pileup on the expressway. An emergency with one of his artists. A flat tire in the rain. There was always something and there always would be. That was just the kind of man he was.

"I'm sorry to hear you're having more trouble with Missy," she said. "But I'm not interested in excuses, Ian.

My father was always full of excuses and apologies. He never blew off school programs or special events on purpose. He wanted to come, but time and time again, his work interfered and he'd promise to make it up to me next time. I don't blame you for being late. At the same time, I don't have to tolerate it, either."

Bree watched a parade of emotions move across Ian's face. Each of them lasted only a second, every one different from the next, leaving her unsure of what he was thinking or feeling. At least until he spoke.

"*Tolerate* it? You don't have to tolerate it?" Ian repeated her words with incredulity. He took a deep breath and ran his fingers through his hair. "You know, that's funny you should say that considering what I've tolerated with you over the past week and a half."

Bree was taken aback by the unexpected assault of words. What had she forced him to tolerate? Her cooking? An unwanted photo session? "With me? Like what?"

"Like your constant needling to change me. You act like you want to be with me, Bree, but you really don't. You want to be with that coffee-shop musician from nine years ago. You practically shoved that guitar into my hands, nagging me until I had no choice but to play or listen to you go on about it. You didn't give a damn how I felt about the whole thing. I had good reasons for not playing that guitar, but you didn't care. When you looked at me, all you saw was this fantasy musician you lost and were desperate to get back. Never mind what I wanted. Never mind what was healthy for me. You wanted what you wanted and you were determined to get your way."

"How dare you! You're acting like I forced you into a life of crime instead of convincing you to face the fact that you're unhappy with your life. You miss your music, but you just won't admit it to yourself because you're afraid to play and fail again. Don't pin your insecurities on me just because I've been successful. I told you the other night that I didn't love you just because of your music. I love you for you and I just wanted you to be happy again. I'm sorry if that makes me into some kind of harpy."

Ian flinched at her words, his gaze narrowing at her. "Yeah, Bree," he said at last with a mocking bitterness underlying his words. "I'm sure you're only interested in my mental health and well-being."

Bree could feel her entire face flush in anger. Her heart pumped furiously in her chest, making the sound of her blood racing in her ears almost deafening. She glanced around the room and noticed that everyone was gone now. She didn't know if they'd left on their own or the scene she was causing with Ian had made them uncomfortable and driven them away. She supposed it didn't matter at this point. It was better not to have an audience for this, anyway.

"You know, my father made it tonight," she said. "The King of Emergencies. The Duke of Last-Minute Meetings. He was here for once in his life. On time. He sat through the entire introduction of me and my work, staying around to look at every picture. When he left tonight, he told me he was so glad he could be here and how proud he was of me."

Ian didn't respond to that. He just stood there, watching her with a tightly clenched jaw.

"And sitting here, alone, I realized how pathetic it was that I was so pleased he came. Somehow it negated the twenty-eight years he missed. And it shouldn't have, but I wanted his approval so badly. I wanted him here for my big showing. That's all I wanted from you."

Ian swallowed hard, considering her words. "I'm sorry I couldn't be here for you tonight. I'm here now. I brought you flowers. I was prepared to..." His voice trailed off and he shook his head. "It doesn't matter. Apparently that's just not good enough. You know, all I ever wanted from you was to be accepted the way I am. Most people would be pleased with a wealthy, successful businessman, but not you. No matter what I do, I'm never good enough. I got enough of that from my father and my college advisors. I certainly don't need it from you."

Bree felt a momentary hitch in her chest. "You are good enough, Ian. You're more than good enough. You are an exceptional person. The only person who doesn't believe it is you, but how can I convince you of that when all you hear are criticisms?"

"So you're saying it's my own fault I feel like a loser? Thanks, Bree. That really helps."

"No! I would never—"

Ian held up his hand to interrupt her. "No. It's okay. You're allowed to feel however you want to feel. But know that we're adults now. We're not kids anymore. And adults have responsibilities. *I* have responsibilities. I would've loved to have been here with you tonight, but it just didn't happen. I had to do what I could to protect my employees, my artists and their families. Instead of standing here looking at some amazing pictures, I was being threatened by a woman who wants to take away everything I've worked years to build. I'm sorry if you don't agree with my priorities, but I had to make a decision and that's what I chose."

For a moment, Bree wanted to stop the fight and

find out what happened with Missy. This had obviously been more than her usual diva hissy fit. But she didn't get the chance.

Ian gestured toward his throat. "I've had it up to here with criticism today. We're obviously fighting an uphill battle. I don't have the time or the energy to waste on this…because I'm so busy," he said, bitterly mocking her criticisms. "You can't accept me the way I am, so I guess you're right about us going our separate ways tonight. There's no point in this relationship going any further."

Bree felt a sharp pain in her chest, as though he'd finally driven the dagger into her heart. It knocked the wind out of her, took away whatever fight she had left. Despite what she said, she didn't want to lose him, even if it was for the best. She was broken. "Fine," she said quietly, her lips nearly trembling with the tears she was struggling to hold back.

Ian nodded, his expression solemn, his green eyes moving over her face without really seeing anything. "Congratulations on your showing tonight. I'm sure it was well received. Good luck with your future endeavors."

At that, Ian turned and walked out.

Bree watched him go, then slumped back down onto the bench. This night was good and truly ruined.

Eleven

"Are you just going to sit around the house all day?"

Ian looked up from his long-standing perch on the couch to see his housekeeper, Winnie, glaring at him through the doorway. She had a vacuum at her side and a look of disgust on her face. That wasn't good. He was obviously cramping her style.

"Maybe," he said, being honest. He didn't have plans to get off this couch anytime soon. He was just going to sit here until he figured out what do to. So far, no luck. Perhaps he should have taken off more than two days from work. "Why?"

The older woman walked into the room and crossed her arms over her chest. "Well, I have things to do and for once you're actually underfoot. You don't pay me to just sit around and watch you mope."

Ian's brow went up at Winnie's sharp tone. "I'm not stopping you from working. Just vacuum around me.

Or clean the other four-thousand square feet I'm not occupying. And I'm *not* moping," he added.

"Sure you're not. You're home in your pajamas instead of at work in a suit. You're strumming your guitar and playing moody songs instead of guiding the careers of your artists. Not to mention that I found *fifteen* candy bar wrappers in the trash can this morning. Tell me you're not moping."

Ian looked at Winnie and frowned. Had he really eaten that many? So maybe he *was* moping. So what? "I've had a rough couple of weeks. Am I not allowed to take a little time to deal with all of it?"

Winnie came over to the couch and sat beside him. "Of course you are, Ian. I can't imagine what you've been through with Missy and then, so soon after, with Bree. I'm just worried because I've never seen you like this. Not in the five years I've worked for you. Not even after you found out Missy was pregnant—and don't bother trying to tell me you were happy about that because I know you weren't.

"You've been as precise as Swiss clockwork for the past five years and it wasn't until now that you've gotten me worried." Winnie gestured toward the guitar. "I didn't even know you played the guitar, Ian. I've been cleaning this place all these years and have never run across one. Or sheet music. Or a picture or anything that would make me think you even played an instrument. Where did this one come from?"

"From the mountain house. I brought it home with me. This is the guitar I bought myself when I was thirteen."

"Why haven't you ever played music around here before?"

"I gave it up when I dropped out of school and started working for the record company."

"Why?"

Ian sighed. He'd just been through all this with Bree. He didn't really want to rehash it, especially because now he realized it had been the wrong choice and justifying his actions was more difficult. "Because I wasn't any good."

"That's funny," Winnie noted. "You've sounded pretty good to me."

"Thanks, Winnie." Ian wasn't fishing for a compliment, but he appreciated it, anyway. It made him feel good to have someone other than Bree tell him that, even though Winnie's praise felt more like that of a mother.

"So what's changed that you're playing again all of a sudden? Wait," she said, "let me guess. It's about Bree."

He nodded. "She encouraged me to start up again. I used to play when we were dating in college."

"Well, she was right," Winnie said. "You're good. You should play more often."

Ian sighed. "I just don't have the time, Winnie. You know I'm always working. I'm either at the studio or working here in my office."

"What about when you were snowed in all that time? Did the world unravel?"

"No," he admitted.

"Did your well-trained employees handle everything while you were away?"

"Yes." Keith had gone above and beyond, as had several others at the studio. He'd already put in some paperwork with payroll to give them bonuses. They deserved it.

"So why do you have to do everything?"

That made Ian frown. It was his company. Why wouldn't he? "What do you mean?"

"You have worked yourself to the bone for years building this label. You've achieved success. Things are going well. You don't have to work as hard anymore. You've just admitted that you have competent staff. Why not take a step back? Let them take on greater responsibility?"

"I'm not just going to sit back—"

"I'm not suggesting you stop going in to the office," Winnie interrupted. "I'm suggesting that you don't have to be responsible for everything. You always put work first because you think that's the only way to be successful. But you're allowed to have a life outside of the office. If that life includes music or a family, great. And even if you just spend all your free time in the bathtub playing with rubber duckies, it's up to you. But don't waste any more time telling yourself you can't do it."

She was right. He paid her to help run his life, to almost fill the role of a wife, and she did it well. She was an incredible cook, she was well organized and she was an excellent sounding board. He didn't know how many times he'd solved a problem by talking it over with Winnie while she cooked or ironed clothes. He needed to give Winnie a raise, too. He'd get his accountant on that immediately.

Winnie patted him on knee. "I've seen you work miracles with your business over the years, Ian. You can do anything you want. Why can't you do this?"

At that, Winnie leaned in to give him a peck on the cheek, then stood. "Okay, enough with the pep talk. This very special episode of *Blossom* is over. Now, get out of the living room so I can clean."

"Thanks, Winnie," he said with a chuckle. Ian got off

the couch and grabbed the neck of his guitar. He carried it with him into his office. Once inside, he stopped, not quite sure why he'd come in here. He didn't want to open his laptop and get sucked into work. He'd taken today off deliberately. So, then what?

He walked over to his leather executive chair and settled into it. With the guitar across his lap, he strummed it gently and tried to think about what he wanted to do next. He liked his office. For whatever reason, it had good energy and he was able to come up with great ideas when he worked from this space. Perhaps it would shake out some plans today, too.

What he knew was that he had made a mistake with Bree. A critical one. That was what had trapped him on the couch in a state of suspended activity while he tried to figure out what to do about it. He'd relived it in his mind. How he could've changed it. What he could've said to make Bree smile instead of going for the jugular when he was pushed.

The drama with Missy couldn't have been foreseen, but it just as easily could've been one of a dozen different emergencies that cropped up from time to time. The truth was that he could've handled it better.

Now he found himself in a quandary. If it was anyone but Bree, he would bury himself in his work and forget about her. But doing that would just prove her right. And it would leave him alone with nothing to show for his time with her but an old guitar, a broken heart and a diamond engagement ring.

It seemed crazy to have bought her a ring so quickly, but it didn't feel quick with Bree. It felt as though they'd been together forever.

Ian opened his nearest desk drawer and reached inside. He pulled out the small velvet box and opened it to look at the ring. The three-carat oval diamond was encircled with a halo of micro-pavé diamonds and set in a platinum band inset with more micro-pavé diamonds. He'd known it was perfect for Bree the moment he saw it. It was elegant yet playful, a ring that would go just as well with a gown as a pair of jeans and sneakers.

It belonged to her, even though he hadn't given it to her yet. He wanted Bree to have it. And he wanted her to know how much he truly loved her. The problem was that Bree would never feel like she was important. He had to show her how much he cared. How sorry he was about their fight and missing her show. Flashing a diamond wouldn't be enough. She'd look at that as the same kind of bribes her father had always offered.

But words wouldn't do, either. Bree had spent her whole life hearing platitudes and excuses from her father and from Ian back when they dated in school. He could promise her the sun, moon and stars, but it wouldn't mean a damn to her until he handed her a planetary body. Especially after the blowup Sunday night. He'd proved to her that his promises meant nothing, even when he had the best of intentions.

Bree would only believe his actions. So action he would take.

Briana Harper has done what few artists in Nashville have been able to do—capture the heart and soul of a town and its people.

Gretchen held the newspaper in her hand and read Bree's long-awaited review aloud at the Monday-morning business meeting.

Armed with a camera, she was able to see beyond

the rhinestone-studded facade to the indomita-
ble spirit that has long characterized the people
and the ideals of Nashville. I predict this is just
the beginning of a long and successful career for
Ms. Harper.

It had been a week since the showing. The review
had been published in the Sunday paper, but Bree hadn't
been able to read it. She'd brought it into the office for
someone else to read it first. As it turned out, she had
chewed her fingernails to the quick for no reason. The
show had been very well received. Apparently the art
critic had left before Ian showed up and their shouting
match outshined the photography.

Bree's three business partners applauded, making
her cheeks flush with embarrassment.

"An excellent show, my dear," Amelia said. "We
should have champagne instead of Starbucks this morning."

"Champagne at nine in the morning?" Natalie asked,
looking mildly scandalized in her sensible black cashmere sweater.

Amelia just shrugged. She wasn't as bothered by
breaking social norms. "Why not? We have a massive
stock of wines in the other room."

"A celebratory latte is just fine. Thank you for picking them up, Natalie."

"Of course," Natalie said with a polite smile. "It's
Monday."

Routines were routines. As such, Bree set aside the
newspaper and fired up her tablet. It was time to discuss the Williams wedding and talk about upcoming
events. The Williams event had been large and for that,
Bree was thankful. She'd been a wreck the first few

days after her show and her fight with Ian. The wedding had forced her to pull herself together and focus on the intricacies of her work.

She'd like to return to that focus now. Talking about the show would just make her think of how it had ended. She accepted the folded newspaper from Gretchen and laid it on top of her notebook.

"You don't seem very happy with your review, Bree." Amelia was frowning at her.

Bree glanced down at the glowing review and pasted a smile on her face. "Of course I'm happy. I'm thrilled. I couldn't have asked for a better write-up. The Whitman Gallery has already called and asked to keep the collection on display for another week. This could lead to another, possibly bigger, show. And this review should bring in more business for From This Moment, too. It's great promotion."

"We don't need more business," Gretchen noted. "We're booked solid for the next year and a half. We really should've scheduled ourselves a vacation or two in there."

"We get the week between Christmas and New Year's Eve off," Natalie pointed out.

Gretchen nodded. "I'll try to remember that the other fifty-one weeks a year."

"We can take vacations," Natalie argued. "We just have to stagger them. Amelia is going to her high school reunion soon. You could take time off if you wanted to. We just can't all go at once."

Gretchen and Natalie started bickering about the intricacies of their corporate leave policy. Bree tuned out, opening up a digital sticky note and making a list of things she needed to do today. By the time she was done, they'd stopped arguing and the attention shifted to business at last.

They finished up the details about an hour later and Bree was the first to dismiss herself. She needed to get the pictures from the weekend downloaded and start going through them. At the reception alone, she often took five hundred photos, not to mention everything else the day of the ceremony and the rehearsal and dinner the night before.

She was about halfway through the photographs when she heard a gentle knock at her door.

"Come in."

She turned in time to see Amelia with the mail. Bree expected her to just leave anything on her desk, but instead, she shut the door and sat down in her guest chair.

Bree groaned inwardly and spun in her chair to face her. "What do you need? When I get done with these pictures I can help with some sugar flowers if that's it."

Amelia shook her head. "I'm not here because of sugar flowers, Bree, and you know it."

She had avoided any kind of serious discussions with her friends and coworkers since the show. They knew that Ian had finally shown up and they'd broken up, but that was it. She'd been hoping she would make it to her Tuesday-Wednesday weekend without talking about it, but that wasn't going to happen. "So what, then?"

Amelia focused her dark eyes on Bree and started twirling her auburn hair around her index finger. "I don't know the details of what happened last week, but don't think I haven't noticed you avoiding me."

"I haven't been avoiding you," Bree said, but they both knew she was lying. "I've been avoiding…talking about *it*. Not you."

"Well, let's cut to the chase, then. Why didn't you tell me you're in love with Ian?"

"What?" Bree shot up in her chair, nearly spilling the half-consumed latte in her hand.

Amelia put the mail in her lap and crossed her arms over her chest. "Don't play dumb with me. You've had that lovesick look in your eye since you got home from the mountains. And after your show—the tremor from your heart breaking probably registered on the Richter scale."

Bree winced at her words. She thought she'd hidden her pain pretty well and kept up an appropriate level of professionalism at the office, but apparently not. "Is it that obvious?"

"Not necessarily. I just know you well enough to see the turmoil you're trying to hide."

"I'll be fine. Just give me a few days. By the Campbell rehearsal on Friday, I should be right as rain."

"You're not going to get over a broken heart in three days. You're in love. Even if you're hurt, it's going to take time. Tell me what happened."

Bree didn't want to recount the scene, but she did it. It had played over and over in her mind during the past week, so it was easy to retell. "When it's all said and done, I trusted him and gave him my heart and I shouldn't have. I was a fool because he did exactly what I knew he would. It's my own fault. I marched myself up the steps to the gallows and put the noose around my neck. I can't get mad at the hangman for doing his job."

Amelia nodded sadly. She sat quietly for a moment. "So where does that leave you two?"

"We're finished. Over. There's obviously no room for anything in his life but his work, and that must be the way he likes it despite his protests and promises.

If that's his choice, then that's just the way it is. I'm not going to waste energy fighting to be a priority in his life."

"But you still love him," Amelia stated.

Her words made tears threaten in Bree's eyes. She took a deep, cleansing breath, looking up at the ceiling and blinking frantically to keep them from spilling down her cheeks.

"I don't know that I ever stopped. And that's what scares me the most. If I was in love with him for nine years while we were apart, how long will I be in love with him going forward? I can't afford to lose another nine years pining for him. I want to be able to find a healthy romance with someone who thinks I'm important. I want to have a family. I don't want to wake up and be forty with nothing to show for my life but pictures of other people's relationships."

There was a sadness in Amelia's eyes as Bree spoke, convincing her that her friend understood how she felt. For a bridal company, they were four women completely miserable at relationships. Bree had apparently been in love with Ian all these years, so her attempts at dating were failures. Amelia was always searching for the big sweeping romance that might not even exist. Gretchen was more comfortable with her art than with men. And Natalie...she didn't even believe in love. They were a sad group.

"Well, I'm sorry everything went down that way. I promise we won't end up forty and alone. What do you say you and I go out on Wednesday night? We might even be able to talk Gretchen into coming. It might cheer you up to get your mind off things."

Bree's eyes widened. Natalie, Gretchen and Amelia had been her friends long before they were business partners, but over the years, the work had taken over their free time. They hadn't gone out for anything more than a working lunch or vendor meeting for a very long time. To go out for drinks in the evening, just for fun, was almost unheard of anymore. Amelia must really be worried about her.

She sighed. Maybe Amelia was right to be worried. "Okay. That sounds fun," she agreed, although her tone was flat and unconvinced. She would make sure it was fun, whether it took too much wine or the dreaded tequila to loosen her up.

"Great," Amelia said with a bright smile. "I'll let you get back to work. Here's your mail." She dropped a couple items onto her desk and slipped back into the hallway.

After all that, Bree wasn't quite ready to return to shot after shot of someone else's happy, romantic day. Instead, she picked up her mail and sorted through it. There was a thank-you note from a recently married couple who adored their wedding photos, a catalog for a photography supply website where she liked to shop and some junk mail.

The last piece of junk mail caught her eye before she tossed it into the trash. It was a postcard for a bar downtown. She'd never even been to that bar before, so she couldn't imagine how she'd gotten on their mailing list.

Frowning, she flipped over the card. It was advertising a special event on Wednesday. For a moment, her eyes flicked over the words without processing them. Then her heart leaped in her chest and she read it again.

Dollar-beer Wednesdays. No cover charge. Musical entertainment from seven to nine by singer/songwriter Ian Lawson.

That was interesting. She stared at the card for several moments, waiting for her vision to clear and the words to change. When they didn't, she had to come to terms with what it meant. Ian had found a way to make room in his life for his music. It seemed it was easier than making room in his life for her.

With a sigh, she held the postcard out over the trash can and dropped it in with the rest of the junk mail.

Good for him.

Twelve

"She's not coming."

"Relax," Keith assured him and handed him his guitar. "The set doesn't start for ten more minutes. She's coming, even if just out of morbid curiosity."

Ian's talent manager at SpinTrax had stepped in to help Ian kick off his new musical career. At the moment, he was serving as his manager, agent, roadie and moral supporter, and all out of the goodness of his heart. Tonight they were playing for fifty bucks and free beer.

So maybe not entirely out of the goodness of his heart. Keith really liked beer.

"No. She's not going to come," Ian insisted, voicing his fears. "She's too angry with me."

He hadn't gone out on a limb and booked this show *for* her. He'd done it for himself, but if she wasn't here to witness it, it wouldn't feel as important. She was the reason he was here. She planted the seed in his mind, pushed him to think outside of the box he'd forced himself into. She was right, of course. He needed to do this. He couldn't suppress the music inside of him any longer.

His future was full of possibilities tonight. There wasn't a fork in the road; there was a starburst. This show might lead to other bookings or it might be his last performance. He might end up only playing for personal enjoyment. He might land his own record deal. Maybe he'd try focusing on songwriting and see if he could sell his songs for other people to sing. It didn't matter. The point was that he was trying. He was putting himself out there, making time in his life for something other than work.

He thought for certain that no matter how she felt about their relationship, she would come to support his music. Or at the very least, come just to rub it in that she was right. Or outright heckle him from the crowd.

And there was a crowd. More than he'd expected to see. It was a good thing he'd done nothing but practice all week. A few tables were scattered throughout with some people at the bar and others standing near the back. Even with all those people, he knew Bree wasn't here. He'd know the moment she arrived. He could feel it when she was near to him. And right now, all he could feel was sick to his stomach.

"Maybe she'll do what you did and show up three minutes before it's over. It would serve you right," Keith noted.

Ian narrowed his gaze at him. "Whose side are you on?"

Keith smiled. "Yours. I'm trying to distract you from your nerves."

Ian opened his mouth to argue that he wasn't nervous, but that wasn't true. He hadn't performed for more than one person at a time for almost a decade. To go from that to a bar packed with one hundred drunk critics was a little unnerving. More than a little. He was a mess.

Doubts pounded at him from all directions. What was he doing here? He was a record executive. He had no business playing at a bar. He had no business playing *anywhere*. This was going to be a disaster, but he still had a chance to avert it. Would anyone notice if he slipped out the back?

"Maybe this was a mistake."

"The only mistake would be you walking out and pissing off a bunch of people who came for some good music." Keith leaned in and patted him on the shoulder. "You're good. I wouldn't tell you that if it wasn't true."

Ian knew that. He'd personally witnessed Keith destroy the dreams of countless wannabe musicians. If you weren't good enough, he would tell you. That was why he'd gone straight to Keith when he decided to give his music another shot. If he was delusional and Bree was just coddling him, Keith would say as much. Instead, his talent manager had crossed his arms over his chest and narrowed his eyes and when the song was done—he'd smiled. It had been damn stressful, but Keith had liked it.

And now, here Ian was. The small platform in the corner of the bar had a stool, a microphone and an amplifier to plug into his new electric acoustic guitar. They'd done a sound check before most people came into the bar and everything was ready to go.

"It's time. Knock 'em dead," Keith said.

Ian nodded and went up onto the platform. Adjusting his guitar, he scanned the crowd again but still no Bree. He tried not to let that get him down. There were a hundred other people in the bar who expected a good show, whether his ex-girlfriend showed up or not.

Leaning into the microphone, Ian introduced himself and thanked everyone for coming. There were a few rowdy "whoops" from the crowd, but they settled down as soon as he started to play. He opened with his acoustic version of "Layla" to get the crowd warmed up.

Five songs into the set, he looked up and saw a group of women pushing their way over to an empty table near the back. He finished his song and watched them settle in as the crowd applauded. There was a shorter girl with curly dark hair, a fiery redhead, a brunette with a sleek ponytail and a blonde whose face he couldn't see.

It was Bree. In that moment, she turned to look at him, her eyes widening with surprise. Her gaze flicked from him to the redhead. She smacked her friend on the shoulder, her lips moving rapidly with angry words. She tried standing up again, but a woman on each side grabbed her arms and tugged her back into the chair.

Apparently she had not planned to come see him tonight. The redhead had lured her here. He'd have to buy Bree's friend a drink later.

Taking a deep breath, Ian decided to play "I'll Love You Forever" for his next song. It was a risk. If she truly didn't want to sit through his show, this song would push her out the door. If she stayed, she might be receptive to the other tune he had in store for later tonight.

He started in on the song he'd written for her all those years ago. His gaze flicked over her, noting a stiffness in her posture, but she hadn't left. She was listening intently, a drink in her hand. He sang as sincerely as he could, and by the end of the song, she had relaxed with a small smile curling her lips.

The applause for that song was bigger than any other

one so far. Given it was an original they'd never heard before, he felt a boost of confidence surge through him.

"That song," Ian said into the microphone, "was written for my college sweetheart. I promised her that I would love her forever. As many of us know, life can get in the way of our plans. We didn't stay together, but I kept my promise. I have never, ever stopped loving her. Even years later, no other woman has touched my heart the way she does."

Bree's wary blue gaze was focused on him the entire time he spoke. Her expression was painfully neutral, not allowing him insight into what she was thinking or feeling about his words. All he could do was charge forward.

"That lovely lady," Ian continued, "is here tonight. I won't embarrass her by pointing her out, but I wanted everyone to know because this next song is about her, too. It's a new song, one I wrote over the past few weeks that we've been apart. You see, I was an idiot, as the male of the species tends to be, and I screwed up my second chance with her."

In response to his confession there was a rumble in the crowd, punctuated by a woman's loud shout of "Men suck!" from the bar.

Ian laughed, thankful it wasn't Bree who'd shouted it. "Sometimes we do. I won't argue that. Being miserable and alone inspired me to write this song." His gaze traveled back to Bree. "I wrote it in the hopes that she would hear it, realize how much I love her and give me another chance."

Bree's pink lips parted slightly as though she were sucking in a gasp of air. He wasn't quite sure what to think of it. She hadn't rushed into his arms, but she hadn't left. She seemed receptive, even though he'd hurt her. That's all he could ask for.

"If she doesn't, you can come home with me!" another woman shouted from a table on the right.

Ian smiled at her and started strumming his guitar. "Well, thank you, sweetheart. It's always good to have a backup plan," he replied to a chorus of laughter from the crowd. "The song I wrote for her is called 'Love Me Anyway.'"

This was the moment that counted. How Bree received this song would determine how the rest of the night would play out. There were several possible outcomes, the best being walking out of here with Bree forgiving him and agreeing to marry him. The worst, with Bree leaving with her girlfriends and Ian getting drunk and going home with the mouthy brunette.

The song was fast-paced and humorous. It wasn't like any song he'd written before. The lyrics were nothing more than a laundry list of his flaws set to a catchy melody. He was certain Bree was aware of each of them, even if she had been too polite to point them out. He knew he worked too much. He needed help prioritizing his life. He needed to have more fun and less stress. He ate too much junk food. He snored louder than a rabid badger during allergy season. He had weirdly shaped toes. Nobody was perfect. But he loved her more than anything else in the world. The chorus announced that he was a work in progress and then asked her to love him despite all that.

That part earned him a round of applause from the crowd and a smile from Bree. The second verse was more of a risk. It was a list of *her* flaws. She was an emotional live wire. She hogged the covers. She owned a cell phone that had previously belonged to Fred Flintstone. She cheated at Scrabble. She always thought she was right. She was pushy and could nag a man into his grave. Last, she had the ability to see right through him, making him absolutely insane.

But he loved her, anyway.

They were *both* works in progress and he wanted to spend the rest of his life with her no matter how long their lists of flaws became. If they improved over the years and ended up polished like diamonds when they were older, great. But if they just got fat together and bickered over the little things twenty-four hours a day, that was great, too. He just wanted to be with her, just as she was, and he hoped she felt the same way.

Every word was true. As he finished playing the last few chords of the song, he looked up to find Bree smiling through her tears. Bingo.

The crowd stood to applaud the song, blocking his view of her. Shouts of "forgive him" could be heard over the roar. Ian didn't wait for the applause to stop before he left the stage. He unplugged his guitar and stepped down into the sea of people and tables.

His chest was tight with excitement and his brain swirled with scenarios as he finally reached her table. Suddenly, he realized something wasn't right. He was in the right place, but there was no tearful, smiling blonde waiting for him with open arms.

Bree was gone.

Bree had to get out of there. She couldn't breathe. The rush of emotions and the swell of the applause had combined to press against her chest like an anvil. She'd bolted before the other girls could stop her, hitting an emergency exit door and dashing into the alley behind the bar.

The air was cold and stung as it rushed in and out of her lungs, but she didn't care. It was better than being in there. Listening to him tell her how much he loved her and asking if she would do the same. She didn't know what to say. She did love him, despite his weird toes and his workaholic tendencies. She wished she didn't, but she did.

She sagged back against the brick facade of the building, her burgundy leather jacket protecting her from the rough surface. All the energy she had was sucked out by the emotional upheaval, leaving her legs feeling like quivering gelatin as the building held her up. She needed to pull herself together. One of the girls would follow her out here eventually. Standing in an alley sobbing was not healthy.

Bree wiped away her tears and dropped her face into her hands. How had this happened? This was supposed to be a night on the town with her friends to *forget* about Ian. Instead, Amelia had tricked her into coming here, saying she wanted to try this new place she'd seen but with a name she couldn't remember. Bree didn't even realize they were at the same place on the same night until she heard him playing on the small stage. The snoop had read her mail.

Betrayal. She was calling Amelia "Brutus" from now on. A wicked, redheaded meddler! Bree had tried to leave the moment she'd figured out what was going on, hopefully before Ian saw her, but it was no use. Amelia and Gretchen had grabbed her and tugged her into the chair. Gretchen had driven so Bree would have had to call a cab to leave. She'd also have to listen to them complain about her being a coward every day for the next year or so if she'd left.

So she'd stayed. And look what came of it! He'd

bared his heart and soul to a room full of strangers. He'd made her laugh, made her cry and made her question everything. Just when she'd finally seemed to pull herself out of the doldrums.

The emergency exit door opened. Bree expected Natalie or Amelia to step out, but instead, it was Ian.

He was looking amazingly handsome yet casual for his musical debut. His expensive suits were nice, but her heart fluttered at the sight of him in a tight pair of jeans. Tonight, he'd paired dark denim with a black T-shirt that fit every muscle of his ripped upper body like liquid latex had been poured over him.

That thought made her mouth go dry in an instant. She'd already sucked down two drinks since she'd arrived for the same reason. Now, more than ever, she needed to be able to talk, but her tongue was like a dry wad of cotton balls in her mouth.

"Your friends told me you ran out this way." He watched her with curious eyes. "I guess you didn't like the new song."

Bree couldn't speak, but she shook her head. "It… was great," she managed. And it was. The content was poignant. The melody was memorable. The accompaniment was inspired. It was a great song, even if it announced to the world that she was a cover hog and a know-it-all. She supposed that was better than telling everyone she was a world-class belcher.

Ian took a few steps closer, a wary expression lining his face. He looked concerned that she might bolt at any moment. He needn't worry about that. Even if her legs would work, she had no idea where she was and her ancient cell phone couldn't look up a cab company in its Yellow Pages app. She was at Gretchen's mercy.

"But it didn't change anything." His soft words were

defeated. She hated that. Ian was a powerful business-man, master of his universe, yet she felt like she could crush him with the slightest inclination. His words weren't a question. He just assumed that she couldn't forgive him.

"No, it didn't."

Ian's gaze fell to the alley pavement, his shoulders slumping slightly in defeat.

"I still love you just as much as I did before I heard it."

Ian's head shot up, a lock of dark hair falling into his eyes. "What? You love me?"

Bree nodded.

His hands dropped to his sides in aggravation. "Then why the hell did you run? You're giving me heart pal-pitations."

She shook her head. "I don't know. It was all too much at once. I needed fresh air. Space. I needed room to think."

Ian stepped closer, placing his hands at her waist. "Have you had enough time to think?" he asked.

She nodded. "I'm much better now that you're here." Bree rested her hands on his forearms and looked up into the green eyes she'd dreamed about the past few days. There was a difference in his face tonight. Less tightness in his jaw. Less stress drawing lines into his forehead and around his eyes. Even without his phone and his computer in the mountains, his mind had been burdened with the worries of his work and his life.

Tonight there was none of that. He looked…happy. Something had changed in his life since she'd seen him last. Big changes. "What's going on with you, Ian? This isn't the same man from a week ago."

"I've treated myself like one of my artists and given myself a makeover. A *life* makeover."

Bree's brow shot up curiously. "What does a life makeover entail?"

Ian smiled. "Everything. When Missy threatened the label the night of your showing, I realized my business isn't my whole world. I've made it the center of my life, but in the end it didn't matter nearly as much to me as you do. Or my music. Or my mental health. So I hired a business manager to offload a lot from my plate. He's handling the business details while Keith handles the artists. I'm still involved, I still make the big decisions, but I'm not bogged down with the little stuff. It's cut my hours in half."

Bree was stunned by the confession. That was a huge step, one she'd never expected him to make. No wonder he looked as though he didn't have a care in the world. "Are you going into withdrawal yet?"

He shrugged. "I have my moments. I've tried to fill my extra time with my music to keep from getting sucked back in. I've bought some new instruments. I got a baby grand piano and blank sheet music to work on some songs. Keith is acting as my agent for now, but I think I'm going to try to get a full-time agent and see where I can get this to go, if anywhere. I'm just happy to be playing again. I had no idea how badly I missed it in my life until I let it back in. So thank you for that."

Bree didn't know what to say. She'd thought perhaps that tonight was just a little pet project he'd do on the side. Open mic nights every other weekend. Playing his guitar as they sat by the fireplace at his penthouse. She never expected him to try pursuing it profession-ally again. "That's amazing, Ian. I'm so proud of you for taking the leap. I know it's scary, but you're really talented."

He smiled. "Thank you. That show wasn't the scariest thing I did tonight, though."

Bree's brow furrowed in confusion. "What could be scarier than singing to a hundred rowdy drunks?"

"Doing this."

Bree watched as Ian slipped one hand into his pocket and then dropped down onto one knee. Her eyes widened with surprise and realization as the pieces came together in her mind. He was proposing. *Proposing!* Her heart started racing madly in her chest. He looked up at her with dark green eyes so overflowing with love, she felt herself start to choke up.

"Briana Harper, you are the love of my life. I've spent years trying to catch lightning in a bottle again, but no one can compare to you. I want to spend every day of the rest of my life with you. Not with my employees. Not with my money or my fancy, empty apartment. None of that matters if you're not with me.

"If I'm playing music, I want you there to hear it. When you take pictures, I want to be in your wake, hauling all of your equipment. I don't just want you to be my wife—I want you to be an integral part of my life. That means I will try my hardest to make sure you always feel like you're the most important thing in the world to me. Will you do me the honor of marrying me?"

Ian opened up the small velvet box to display the ring he'd chosen for her. She gasped when the streetlights hit the giant diamond inside. It was massive, bigger than anything she could've imagined and nothing like she'd ever seen. Considering she took a lot of engagement ring and wedding ring portraits, that was saying a lot. It was oval and surrounded by tiny diamonds that continued around the band.

It was the most beautiful thing she'd ever seen. And even then, the ring couldn't touch the words that went with it. The man she loved had just promised her everything she'd ever wanted. Not just love, but a lifetime of companionship. Of feeling important, never cast aside when work and other priorities interfered.

"Yes," she whispered through the tears that suddenly started streaming down her cheeks. "I will marry you."

Ian slipped the ring onto her hand with fingers that shook almost imperceptibly. With it placed snugly, he stood and scooped her into his arms. He smiled a wide, contented smile before leaning in to capture her lips with his own.

Bree melted into him, the world suddenly feeling more right than it had in a very long time. Being in his arms, knowing she was an integral part of Ian's future, she could forget anything else happening around them. She even forgot they were in an alley behind a bar until an employee came out and threw a sack of trash into the Dumpster a couple yards away.

That brought them both back to reality. Ian took her hand and led her toward the door so they could share the good news with their hundred new friends. Bree was certain the dark-haired woman in the front would be highly disappointed to know Ian had been snatched up before she got her chance.

"Do you mind if I announce our engagement to the crowd? I think it will get them amped up for the second set."

Bree nodded and leaned in to give him a good-luck kiss. "One condition, though," she added.

His brows went up. "What's that?"

"I want a disclaimer. I don't cheat at Scrabble. You're just a poor loser with a limited vocabulary."

"Fair enough," he said with a smile. "If you'll still marry me, I'll get up there and tell them anything you'd like."

Epilogue

"What about this dress?" Gretchen slid a bridal magazine across the meeting-room table to Bree. "I like the giant silk rosettes at the bottom."

Bree glanced at the picture and wrinkled her nose. "That's a little fussy for me. I want something more simple and timeless. I was thinking more along the lines of this one." She tapped the page and slid her magazine back to Gretchen. "It's ruched ivory organza with a small crystal embellishment at the hip. I'm definitely not in the market for a ball gown. Please keep in mind that I'm wearing sparkly silver Converse under whatever dress I choose."

She expected Amelia to lodge a complaint about her bridal footwear, but her fashionable coworker didn't seem to be listening. She was lost in her own bridal magazine, flipping slowly through the pages but not seeing anything. She seemed like she was a million miles away, a slight frown pulling down the corners of her mouth.

Amelia had been like this since she'd gotten back from her high school reunion nearly a month ago. She'd been excited to go, but she'd returned from her hometown a little quiet and more pensive than usual. Bree thought that graduating in Las Vegas would make for a more exciting reunion, but Amelia hadn't come home excited. She also hadn't come home wanting to talk about it much.

Bree's wedding was a year off at least, so dress shopping wasn't critical, but she thought it might perk up Amelia to look at dresses with her. She'd brought in a stack of magazines for everyone to look over today before their weekly meeting. Amelia loved fashion, and bridal gowns were the epitome of that to her. She couldn't wait to sneak out of the kitchen to see the bride's dress each Saturday.

But Bree's plan hadn't worked. Amelia hadn't said a word all morning as she mindlessly flipped through the pages of the massive bridal magazine.

Bree knew that what happened in Vegas was supposed to stay there, but this was getting ridiculous. "Amelia?"

The redhead snapped her head up, her thoughts finally on the here and now. "What?"

Gretchen and Bree looked at each other and they both frowned. There was something going on and she was going to get to the bottom of it right now. "What is going on with you?"

Amelia's dark eyes widened and she shook her head dismissively. "There's nothing going on with me. I just didn't sleep very well last night."

"Liar," Gretchen accused and crossed her arms

over her chest. "You've been acting funny since you got home from Las Vegas. What happened at your reunion? When I went to mine, all the cheerleaders had gotten fat and all the nerds were rich. I was still the artistic one with the name no one recalled. I had a few drinks, a few laughs with people who didn't remember who I was and I went home. Nothing to lose sleep over."

Amelia twisted her lips in thought but didn't say anything. Whatever it was that had happened, she didn't want to talk about it. That was just too damn bad, Bree decided. She hadn't wanted to go to that bar and hear Ian sing, either. Amelia had forced her, and look how it had turned out. She was getting married. It was time for Amelia to spill about what was bothering her.

"What's the big deal? What could you have possibly done there that's so bad? It's not like you eloped in one of those tacky wedding chapels," Bree argued.

Amelia looked up at her, her eyes suddenly wide with panic. Her mouth dropped open, her lips moving in argument without making any sound.

"Amelia..." Gretchen pressed, "tell me you didn't elope in a Las Vegas wedding chapel."

She took a deep breath and slowly nodded. "I did. The details are a little blurry, but I woke up married to my best friend."

* * * * *

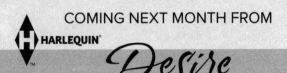

COMING NEXT MONTH FROM

HARLEQUIN
Desire

Available February 3, 2015

#2353 HER FORBIDDEN COWBOY
Moonlight Beach Bachelors • by Charlene Sands
When his late wife's younger sister needs a place to heal after being jilted at the altar, country-and-western star Zane Williams offers comfort at his beachfront mansion. But when he takes her in his arms, they enter forbidden territory...

#2354 HIS LOST AND FOUND FAMILY
Texas Cattleman's Club: After the Storm
by Sarah M. Anderson
Tracking down his estranged wife to their hometown hospital, entrepreneur Jake Holt discovers she's lost her memory—and had his baby. Will their renewed love stand the test when she remembers what drove them apart?

#2355 THE BLACKSTONE HEIR
Billionaires and Babies • by Dani Wade
Mill owner Jacob Blackstone is all business; bartender KC Gatlin goes with the flow. But her baby secret is about to shake things up as these two very different people come together for their child's future...and their own.

#2356 THIRTY DAYS TO WIN HIS WIFE
Brides and Belles • by Andrea Laurence
Thinking twice after a reckless Vegas elopement, two best friends find their divorce plans derailed by a surprise pregnancy. Will a relationship trial run prove they might be perfect partners, after all?

#2357 THE TEXAN'S ROYAL M.D.
Duchess Diaries • by Merline Lovelace
When a sexy doctor from a royal bloodline saves the nephew of a Texas billionaire, she loses her heart in the process. But secrets from her past may keep her from the man she loves...

#2358 TERMS OF A TEXAS MARRIAGE
by Lauren Canan
The fine print of a hundred-year-old land lease will dictate Shea Hardin's fate: she must marry a bully or lose it all. But what happens when she falls for her fake husband...hard?

YOU CAN FIND MORE INFORMATION ON UPCOMING HARLEQUIN® TITLES, FREE EXCERPTS AND MORE AT WWW.HARLEQUIN.COM.

HDCNM0115

REQUEST YOUR FREE BOOKS!
2 FREE NOVELS PLUS 2 FREE GIFTS!

HARLEQUIN

Desire

ALWAYS POWERFUL, PASSIONATE AND PROVOCATIVE

YES! Please send me 2 FREE Harlequin Desire® novels and my 2 FREE gifts (gifts are worth about $10). After receiving them, if I don't wish to receive any more books, I can return the shipping statement marked "cancel." If I don't cancel, I will receive 6 brand-new novels every month and be billed just $4.55 per book in the U.S. or $4.99 per book in Canada. That's a savings of at least 13% off the cover price! It's quite a bargain! Shipping and handling is just 50¢ per book in the U.S. and 75¢ per book in Canada.* I understand that accepting the 2 free books and gifts places me under no obligation to buy anything. I can always return a shipment and cancel at any time. Even if I never buy another book, the two free books and gifts are mine to keep forever.

225/326 HDN F4ZC

Name _____ (PLEASE PRINT)

Address _____ Apt. #

City _____ State/Prov. _____ Zip/Postal Code

Signature (if under 18, a parent or guardian must sign)

Mail to the **Harlequin® Reader Service:**
IN U.S.A.: P.O. Box 1867, Buffalo, NY 14240-1867
IN CANADA: P.O. Box 609, Fort Erie, Ontario L2A 5X3

Want to try two free books from another line?
Call 1-800-873-8635 or visit www.ReaderService.com.

* Terms and prices subject to change without notice. Prices do not include applicable taxes. Sales tax applicable in N.Y. Canadian residents will be charged applicable taxes. Offer not valid in Quebec. This offer is limited to one order per household. Not valid for current subscribers to Harlequin Desire books. All orders subject to credit approval. Credit or debit balances in a customer's account(s) may be offset by any other outstanding balance owed by or to the customer. Please allow 4 to 6 weeks for delivery. Offer available while quantities last.

Your Privacy—The Harlequin® Reader Service is committed to protecting your privacy. Our Privacy Policy is available online at www.ReaderService.com or upon request from the Harlequin Reader Service.

We make a portion of our mailing list available to reputable third parties that offer products we believe may interest you. If you prefer that we not exchange your name with third parties, or if you wish to clarify or modify your communication preferences, please visit us at www.ReaderService.com/consumerchoice or write to us at Harlequin Reader Service Preference Service, P.O. Box 9062, Buffalo, NY 14269. Include your complete name and address.

HD13R

Separated and on the verge of divorce, Jake Holt is determined to confront his wife. But when he arrives in Royal, Texas, he finds that Skye has been keeping secrets...

Jake had spent the past four years pointedly not caring about what his family was doing. They'd wanted him to put the family above his wife. Nothing had been more important to him than Skye.

He was not staying in Royal long. Just enough to get Skye back on her feet and figure out where they stood.

Just then, the baby made a little hiccup-sigh noise that pulled at his heartstrings.

Jake's brother picked the baby up so smoothly that Jake was jealous.

"Grace, honey—this is your daddy," Keaton said as he rubbed her back. Then, to Jake, he added, "You ready?"

Not really—but Jake wasn't going to admit that to Keaton. He tried to cradle his arms in the right way. Then Keaton laid the baby in them.

The world seemed to tilt off its axis as Jake looked down into his daughter's eyes. They were a pale blue—

just like her mother's. Up close now, he could see that Grace had wispy hairs on her head that were so white and fine they were almost see-through.

She didn't start bawling, which he took as a good sign. Instead, she waved her tiny hands around, so of course he had to offer her one of his fingers. When she latched on to it, he felt lost and yet *not* lost at the same time.

He was responsible for this little girl from this moment until the day he drew his last breath. The weight of it hit him so hard that if he hadn't already been sitting, his knees would have buckled.

This was his daughter. He and Skye had created this little person.

God, he wished Skye was here with him. That things between them had been different. That he'd been different.

But he couldn't change the past, not when his present—and his future—was gripping his little finger with surprising strength.

Don't miss what happens next in
HIS LOST AND FOUND FAMILY
by Sarah M. Anderson!

Available February 2015,
wherever Harlequin® Desire books and ebooks are sold.